THE CHALLENGE

They started on their way back to the wagon. When they got to it, they saw a man sitting on the wagon seat. Slocum did not know the man, but there was a familiar look about him. He was almost sure the man was a Hemp. They stopped on the board sidewalk a few feet away. Slocum noticed the man wore two guns.

"Micah Hemp," said Merilee.

"What the hell are you doing on our wagon?" said Morton.

"I was just setting here waiting on you all," said Micah.

"I reckon you mean you were waiting on me," said Slocum.

"If you be Slocum," said Micah.

"I'm Slocum."

"Then I'm waiting here to kill you."

"There's no need for it," said Slocum.

"You've killed two Hemps," said Micah. "That's need enough and more."

"They both drew on me," said Slocum.

"I don't know about that, and I don't care. I'm fixing to climb down off of this here wagon. You can go for your gun anytime after I get down."

"I don't even know you," Slocum said as Micah hauled himself down from the wagon and strode to the middle of the sidewalk. "I ain't going to pull on you."

"Then I'll just kill you like a dog . . ."

JAKE LOGAN

SLOCUM
AND THE
BIG PAYBACK

J

JOVE BOOKS, NEW YORK

THE BERKLEY PUBLISHING GROUP
Published by the Penguin Group
Penguin Group (USA) Inc.
375 Hudson Street, New York, New York 10014, USA
Penguin Group (Canada), 90 Eglinton Avenue East, Suite 700, Toronto, Ontario M4P 2Y3, Canada
(a division of Pearson Penguin Canada Inc.)
Penguin Books Ltd., 80 Strand, London WC2R 0RL, England
Penguin Group Ireland, 25 St. Stephen's Green, Dublin 2, Ireland (a division of Penguin Books Ltd.)
Penguin Group (Australia), 250 Camberwell Road, Camberwell, Victoria 3124, Australia
(a division of Pearson Australia Group Pty. Ltd.)
Penguin Books India Pvt. Ltd., 11 Community Centre, Panchsheel Park, New Delhi—110 017, India
Penguin Group (NZ), Cnr. Airborne and Rosedale Roads, Albany, Auckland 1310, New Zealand
(a division of Pearson New Zealand Ltd.)
Penguin Books (South Africa) (Pty.) Ltd., 24 Sturdee Avenue, Rosebank, Johannesburg 2196,
South Africa

Penguin Books Ltd., Registered Offices: 80 Strand, London WC2R 0RL, England

This is a work of fiction. Names, characters, places, and incidents either are the product of the author's imagination or are used fictitiously, and any resemblance to actual persons, living or dead, business establishments, events, or locales is entirely coincidental.

SLOCUM AND THE BIG PAYBACK

A Jove Book / published by arrangement with the author

PRINTING HISTORY
Jove edition / April 2006

ISBN: 0-515-14121-6

JOVE®
Jove Books are published by The Berkley Publishing Group,
a division of Penguin Group (USA) Inc.,
375 Hudson Street, New York, New York 10014.
JOVE is a registered trademark of Penguin Group (USA) Inc.
The "J" design is a trademark belonging to Penguin Group (USA) Inc.

PRINTED IN THE UNITED STATES OF AMERICA

10 9 8 7 6 5 4 3 2 1

1

Slocum was running a string of bad luck. He had a few dollars in his pocket and a couple of cigars left, but that was about all. His last job had paid him pretty well, but he had wandered around since then for some time. He had not worked during that time, and had spent most of his money. He was beginning to feel the need of another job, or at least the need to make some more money. He did not like the prospect of being broke. He enjoyed his good cigars and good whiskey much too much for that, and he could see that a few days in this jerkwater town would bring him to the point where his pockets were empty much too soon.

The town was called Hard Luck, and Slocum was hoping that the name was no indication of what was waiting for him there. He found the Hard Luck Saloon, not a difficult job at all, and he had made his way in there in the midst of a pretty good crowd. The customers must have come from nearby ranches or something, he figured, because he could not imagine that the town had so many residents. There were three poker games running at tables around the room, but they did not attract him. His money would be gone soon enough without that kind of activity. Most of the tables were taken up, so he bellied up to the bar and ordered a shot of whiskey. His Appaloosa was already stabled for the night, so he had no other worries. He figured even if he spent all his money in that place, he could always sleep outside somewhere. He had done plenty of that in his lifetime.

He drank his whiskey and ordered a second shot. He checked his cash and found that he had enough for a couple more shots, a room for the night, and breakfast in the morning, so he settled his mind that two more shots would do it. He would let lunch worry about itself when the time came. He heard a ruckus start up at the far end of the room, so he glanced that way. Two cowhands were duking it out jostling the crowd. The customers at that end of the room spread out and gave them space. Most of the people in the room were watching the fight. The card players at the three tables ignored it and kept playing their games. A man was on the way up the stairs with a saloon woman, and they stopped halfway up to watch the fight.

Slocum turned away and finished his drink, but when he went to order a third, he found that the bartender, like most everyone else, was intent on watching the cowhands pound one another. There was no way Slocum could get his attention. He had no choice left then but to watch the fight, wishing it would end so he could get another drink. The combatants were on the floor by this time. He couldn't see them, but he had no trouble hearing the shot ring out. Everything suddenly got still and quiet. Even the fighters stopped. Slocum saw a man with a star on his chest pushing his way through the crowd, a six-gun in his right hand.

"Aw, Hardy," someone said, "let them fight it out."

"Shut up," said the man called Hardy. "All right, you two. Get up off the floor."

Through the crowd, Slocum could see the two bloody heads as the men stood up.

"I'm going to give you two choices," Hardy said. "You

can get the hell out of town right now or spend the night in my jail."

"I'll go," said one of the men.

"Me, too," said the other.

The crowd parted enough for the two men to walk through and get to the door. Slocum watched as they went out. People started moving back to their places at the tables or at the bar. Talk resumed. Hardy holstered his weapon and stood watching, as if to make sure that no more trouble broke out in the place. Slocum was able to get the attention of the barkeep and order another drink. Sheriff Hardy left the saloon. Just then Slocum caught a glimpse of a face that seemed familiar to him. One of the men who had been watching the fight had just returned to his seat at a table behind Slocum, and Slocum saw his face in the mirror behind the bar. It took him a couple of seconds to register the face. It was Asa Hemp, wanted for murder. There was no question. Slocum tried to remember the dodger he had seen on the man. He tried to recall the amount of the reward that was offered for him.

It didn't much matter. Any amount would be that much more than he had in his pockets just then. He thought for a moment. Bounty hunting was not the most attractive job in the world to Slocum, but he was nigh onto being desperate. The Hard Luck Saloon would not be a good place to try to collect the reward, though, because it was much too crowded. He decided to wait the man out. Sooner or later he would have to leave the place. Slocum kept his eye on the man in the mirror. He was drinking heavily. If nothing else, he would have to go out to take a leak soon, Slocum thought. He slowed down, sipping his third whiskey.

A saloon woman squeezed in beside Slocum and put a hand on his shoulder. "Buy a girl a drink, cowboy?" she said.

"Not now," said Slocum.

"You a tightwad?" she said.

"Just damn near broke, darlin'."

"Hunh," she snorted, and she turned away to look for another victim.

It was none too soon, for just then, Hemp stood up and walked toward the back door. Slocum waited for a moment, then followed him. He had to jostle his way through the crowd, and when he got to the back door and walked through it to the outside, there was no sign of Hemp. Four men lounged against the back wall sharing a bottle, and an outhouse stood not far away. Slocum assumed that Hemp had gone in there. He leaned against the wall to wait. The four men looked at him suspiciously, but he ignored them. In another moment the outhouse door was opened, and Hemp stepped out, still fastening up his britches. Slocum stepped away from the wall.

"Asa Hemp?" he said.

Hemp stopped still and looked up. "Who wants to know?"

"My name's Slocum, and I'm arresting you for murder."

"You a lawman?"

"This is a citizen's arrest."

"A bounty man, huh?"

"Call it what you like. Throw down your gun and come with me to the sheriff's office."

"I ain't gonna do that," said Hemp. A mean snarl crossed his face.

"That's your choice," Slocum said.

"What'd you call yourself? Slocum?"

"That's right."

"I've heard of you."

"What've you heard?"

"You're fast," Hemp said. "Real fast."

"Then maybe you'd best throw down your gun and come along with me peaceful."

"Well, I don't know what you've heard about me, but I'm real fast, too."

"You want to find out by dying?"

"It might be you doing the dying, Slocum."

"Make up your mind, Hemp," Slocum said. "Throw down your gun or else use it."

"Hold on a minute, Slocum. You're a stranger here, so maybe you ain't heard. This is my town. You put me in jail, they might have a trial, but they'll never find twelve men who will convict me."

"Then make it easy on yourself. Come along with me to the jail."

"Maybe I don't want to spend a night in jail. Maybe I don't want to let folks around here see me took in like that. Maybe I just want to find out which one of us is the best."

"It's your play," said Slocum.

Suddenly Hemp's right hand flashed toward his six-gun. Slocum made his move as well. Hemp's bullet smashed into the wall behind Slocum as Slocum stepped aside and fired. Slocum's slug hit Hemp in the center of the chest. Hemp stood still for a moment looking down, surprised. A dark splotch appeared in the middle of his chest and slowly spread. His fingers relaxed, and his gun fell from his hand. He took an uneasy step forward, then staggered back two steps and fell with a thud. Slocum holstered his gun and glanced over at the four men.

"One of you boys go get the sheriff," he said.

The four men looked at one another, and then one of them took off at a run. Slocum sat down on the step outside the back door to the Hard Luck Saloon. He took a cigar out of his pocket and lit it with a Lucifer match. No one said anything until the sheriff appeared. For a moment Sheriff Hardy stood and stared at the body. At last he looked up at Slocum still sitting and puffing. "You do this?" he asked.

"I did."

"It didn't take you long to get in trouble here, did it?"

Slocum stood up slowly. "I don't see how I'm in any trouble," he said. He jerked a thumb toward the body. "This man was wanted for murder. A reward's been posted on him."

Hardy looked toward the four men still lounging against the wall. "You boys carry him over to Elmo's place, will you?"

"Sure," one of them said, and they all moved to pick up the corpse and carried it away. Hardy watched them until they had disappeared around the corner of the saloon. Then he looked at Slocum again.

"Well," he said, "why don't you walk on over to my office with me?"

Slocum followed Hardy back into the saloon, through the big room to the front door and out again onto the board sidewalk and down to the next block. Hardy opened a door to the sheriff's office and stepped aside. Slocum hesitated a moment, then stepped in. Hardy followed and shut the door. Then he walked around behind his desk and sat down. He gestured toward a chair, and Slocum took it.

"You got some papers for me to sign?" Slocum asked.

"Papers? Oh. You mean for the reward?"

"What else would I be meaning?"

Hardy opened a desk drawer and took out some papers, tossing them on the desk in front of himself. "Yeah," he said, "we could do that, if you really want to."

"Sheriff," said Slocum, "I ain't a regular bounty man, but I been riding a streak of bad luck. I'm damn near broke. Now, that man was worth some money, and I earned it. I mean to collect it."

"Let me tell you something— What's your name?"

"Slocum."

"Well, let me tell you something, Slocum. I knew Asa Hemp. Knew him real well. I knew about the charges against him and about the reward. But I didn't bother him, and he didn't break the law around here."

"That sounds like a real comfortable arrangement for the both of you," Slocum said.

"I ain't through," said Hardy. "Asa grew up in this town. His whole family lives here, and it's a big family. Just as soon as they hear what happened, they'll be coming in from their ranch. They'll be looking for you. You're going to have to kill about ten men to survive this deal."

"Just let me sign those papers and pay me my money," said Slocum, "and I'll be riding on."

"We can fill out the papers and sign them all right," Hardy said, "but I can't pay you. I have to send them off, and it'll be about ten days before your money shows up. That's ten days of dealing with the Hemps. Well, it might not take them ten days. They'll likely get you tomorrow if you're just hanging around town. You reckon that's worth two thousand dollars?"

"Sheriff," said Slocum, "I didn't set out to kill the son of a bitch. I asked him kindly to take a walk down here to your office with me. He said you couldn't get a jury together around these parts that would convict him, so I told him again to go on to jail with me. What the hell did he have to lose? Well, just his pride, I guess. He went for his gun, but I got him first. Now I want my money. Two thousand, you say? That ain't bad. Let's do that paperwork. I'll be here in ten days to get paid."

"It's like talking to a damn fence post," said Hardy, as he picked up a pen and dipped it in a bottle. In a few minutes, the chore was done. Slocum headed for the door. Just as he jerked it open, Hardy said, "I'll have your money here in ten days, Slocum, but I don't look for you to be here to collect it."

Out on the sidewalk Slocum stood for a spell trying to think what to do. He had thought earlier that he would take a room in the local hotel, named the Hard Luck Hotel, get a good night's sleep, get up in the morning and have a good breakfast. He hadn't thought much beyond that. Now he wasn't so sure about even that much. Ten men, the sheriff had said, out on a ranch. Slocum wondered how far out the ranch was, how long it would take for word to get to them and then for them to get to town. Would they all come at once? He finally decided to go back to the Hard Luck Saloon and have one more drink. Then he would get his horse out of the stable and ride out of town. He could survive out on the prairie for ten days with no problem. Then he could figure out how to slip back into town for his money. It wasn't the greatest plan in the world, but it was the best he could think of on the spur of the moment.

He walked back down the sidewalk until he came to the saloon, and then he went inside. It was about as crowded as before, but he noticed that when he came in, the voices all died down to a murmur. The word was already around. He shouldn't have been surprised at that. He had killed the man just behind the saloon. Everyone had heard the shot, and the four men who had carried the body away had most likely come back to tell the tale. He watched in the mirror very closely as he moved up to the bar. The bartender came over with a sour look on his face.

"Whiskey," Slocum said.

The bartender poured him a drink and took his money without a word. Then he walked away again, to visit with some cowboys a few feet down the bar away from Slocum. Slocum took a sip of the whiskey. Watching in the mirror, he could see no suspicious movements, but he could also see all eyes on him, all that is except those of the poker players at the three tables. Nothing bothered them. Slocum finished his drink and walked outside, turning to head for the stable. He had gone but a few feet when he heard footsteps behind him, and a voice called out, "Hey, mister."

Slocum whirled, pulling out his Colt, and he saw a young cowhand back on the sidewalk throw his hands up in the air.

"Hey, don't shoot," the cowhand said.

Slocum stood still. "What do you want?" he said.

"I just want to talk," said the cowhand. "That's all. My name's Carl Doaks. Okay?"

Slocum studied Doaks for a moment. Then he holstered his Colt, and Doaks came up closer. "I, uh, I heard what you did," he said.

"It appears everyone heard," said Slocum.

"Yeah. Word of a shooting travels fast. 'Specially the shooting of a Hemp."

"You ain't a Hemp, are you?"

"No, sir. Like I said, my name's Carl Doaks. I run a little spread south of town. Hardscrabble outfit. I got one ole boy that works for me, name of Sam Halter. That's all. We just barely hang on, but it's better than nothing. To help make ends meet, I used to work for the Hemps, but I couldn't get along with them, so I quit. They got a big ranch north of town. We don't see each other too much, and when we do, we ain't got nothing to say to each other."

"So what did you call out to me for?" asked Slocum.

"I was just wondering, are you getting out of town? 'Cause it seems to me that's a good idea."

"That's just what the sheriff told me," Slocum said. "I've got a reward coming to me, and I mean to collect it, but I figure that I'll wait it out somewhere besides in town."

"Yeah, It might be healthier. Say, me and ole Sam, we kind of get on each other's nerves some. It might be good for us to have someone else around for a spell. How'd you like to come out to my place? You could stay for as long as you need to. No one would know you're around."

"How come you're making me this offer?"

"To tell you the truth, I'm kind of glad you done what you done. Those Hemps get away with way too much around here. They have for a long time now. What do you say?"

"I'll work for my stay," Slocum said.

"You don't have to."

"I will."

Doaks shrugged and held out his hand. Slocum shook it.

"It's settled then," said Doaks. "You got a horse?"

"In the stable."

"Mine's just back yonder on the street. I'll get him and meet you there." As Slocum headed for the stable and Doaks turned back toward where his mount waited at the hitchrail, a pair of watery eyes watched them from the darkness between two buildings.

2

The sleazy man from the shadows crept out into the open as he saw the two mounted men ride out of Hard Luck together, going toward the Doaks ranch. He took the makings out of his pocket and rolled himself a smoke. Striking a match on the wall, he fired up the cigarette and inhaled deeply. As he started to exhale, he was seized by a fit of coughing. When it finally subsided, he took another drag on the cigarette. There were tears running down his face from the coughing fit, and he wiped them with a sleeve of his shirt. Then he started walking toward the Hard Luck Saloon. He walked inside and over to the bar, where he ordered a shot of whiskey. He coughed some while he waited for the barkeep to fetch it. Then he drank it down at once and started to cough some more. The barkeep stood watching him. When he stopped coughing and stood leaning weakly on the bar, the barkeep said, "Want another, Jackson?"

"Hell, no, Brace," said the man with the watery eyes and the terrible cough, "I gotta go. I got work to do."

He turned and left the saloon, coughing as he did. He found his horse, still saddled and waiting patiently at the hitchrail where he had left it some time earlier, and he mounted up and turned it in the opposite direction from the way in which Slocum and Doaks had ridden out. He rode hard at first, and then he slowed down. It was as if his excitement started him out, and then he had time to think about what he was doing. It was a little too far out to the Hemp ranch to ride that hard. So he took it easy on the horse. He rolled another cigarette as he made his way out to see the Hemps, and he coughed as he rode.

Slocum and Doaks pulled up in front of a long, low building. It was ranch house, bunkhouse and cook shack all in one. There was a corral off to one side that contained six horses. Doaks and Slocum turned their own mounts loose in the corral after taking off their saddles. Then they went inside, and Doaks pointed out a bunk that Slocum could make use of.

"You hungry?" Doaks asked.

"Naw, I had something in town a little earlier. Thanks."

Doaks went to a cabinet on one wall and pulled out a bottle of whiskey and two glasses, holding them up for Slocum to see.

"Well, now," said Slocum, "that looks tempting."

Doaks took the glasses to a table and poured them full, setting the bottle on the table, too. Slocum walked over to join him, and they both sat down. Just then they heard the sound of an approaching horse. "I reckon that'll be Sam," said Doaks. "Sam Halter, my hand."

"Oh, yeah," said Slocum. Still, he moved his chair around a bit so that no one could walk up behind him, and he checked to be sure that his Colt was hanging where he could get to it easily. In another couple of minutes, the door opened and a cowhand walked in. He looked up, surprised to see Slocum.

"Got a visitor, Boss?" Halter said.

"Got a new hand, for a spell anyhow," said Doaks. "Come on over here and say howdy to Slocum."

Halter looked suspiciously from Doaks to Slocum, but he walked to the table and shook hands with Slocum. "Slocum, huh?" he said.

"That's right," said Slocum.

Doaks walked over to the cabinet and got another glass. He brought it to the table and poured it full. Then he re-filled the other two and sat down. "Come on, Sam," he said. "Sit down and join us."

Sam sat and took a drink, but he had a sour expression on his face. "Carl," said Halter, "you didn't say nothing about looking for another hand."

"Well, I wasn't exactly looking," said Doaks. "I just kinda met Slocum in town, and it seemed like the right thing to do."

"Well, I guess it ain't none of my business," said Halter, "but—"

"Sam, listen to this," said Doaks. "Slocum shot and killed Asa Hemp. He needed a place to lay low for about ten days, and I offered him the ranch."

"Killed Asa Hemp," said Halter. "That sounds like trouble to me."

"Forget it, Sam. I invited Slocum out here to stay with us because I like seeing someone stand up to any one of those Hemps. I don't think that anyone knows he's out here, but even so, if it means a little trouble, so be it. Fuck them."

Jackson rode up to the front porch of the big ranch house at the Hemp spread. He was about to dismount, but a ranch hand appeared on the porch with a rifle in his hands. "Just hold it right there," he said.

"I got business," said Jackson, but he started coughing, and it seemed to him, and likely to the cowhand with the rifle, that the fit would never subside. It finally did, though, and Jackson tried again. "I got business with Elihu," he said.

"Tell me about it," said the cowhand.

"I don't talk to no one but Elihu," said Jackson.

Another cowhand came walking around the corner of the house, and the first one walked over to him and whispered in his ear. The second cowhand went into the house. A few minutes went by, and then the cowhand came back out. "He's coming," he said. Jackson started coughing again, and the front door opened again. Elihu Hemp came walking out. He was a barrel of a man, thick chested, with large arms and legs and a neck like a bull. He wore a full beard trimmed close to the skin, and high, black leather boots with his trouser legs tucked down inside them. He had on a white shirt and a vest, but he had already pulled off his suit coat and tie, and the vest was unbuttoned. He carried a bottle and two glasses, and he set them on a table there on the porch. He waited until Jackson's fit passed.

"Hello, Jackson," he said. "What brings you around?"

"I got some big news for you," said Jackson. "I'm afraid it ain't good." He fell into another coughing fit.

"Come up here, Jackson," said Elihu, as soon as he could make himself heard. "This will be good for you." He poured a glass full of whiskey. Jackson made his way up the steps and sat down at the table, taking up the glass at once and draining it. He put the empty glass down on the table and sat with his head down, breathing hard for another moment. At last he spoke.

"Elihu," he said, "Asa got hisself killed in town today."

"Asa?" said Elihu. He stood up and paced away from the table, to the far end of the porch, where he stood and stared out into the darkness for what seemed to Jackson an eternity. At last he turned and walked back to the table, where he sat down again and poured another glass of whiskey for Jackson. "Tell me about it," he said.

"It was a stranger in town," said Jackson. "I never did catch his name, but he was a bounty hunter. I could tell that. He tried to arrest Asa right there in the Hard Luck Saloon. Well, you know Asa. He wouldn't go for that. He did go for his gun, though, but the stranger beat him. He was fast, Elihu. I ain't never seen none faster." Jackson started to cough. It was a hard fit, and he wound up with his head between his knees. At last he stopped, and he wiped his eyes and face with his shirtsleeve. "Anyhow," he said finally, "Sheriff Hardy told him he'd have to stick around for ten days before he could collect the reward money. Carl Doaks invited him to stay out to the ranch with him."

"Doaks did that?" said Elihu.

"I seen them ride out of town together," said Jackson. He coughed a couple of times.

Elihu stood up and reached into a pocket for some change. He brought out a ten-dollar gold piece, which he tossed on the table in front of Jackson. "You can sleep in the bunkhouse tonight if you want to, Jackson," he said. "Take that bottle with you. I appreciate you coming out here."

Jackson stood up clutching the gold piece first and then taking the bottle by its neck. "I was glad to do it, Elihu," he said, and then he started coughing. Elihu was glad for the fit. It gave him a chance to get away.

"Go on over to the bunkhouse, Jackson," he said. "I'll talk to you later." Without waiting for Jackson to survive this fit, Elihu went back inside the house. "Emilie," he called out. "Darling. Would you gather up my brothers for me? We need to have us a serious talk."

"What's it about, dear?" said Emilie. She was maybe thirty years old, certainly no more than that. A beautiful red-haired woman, she was also dressed graciously, right out of a fashion catalogue.

"I don't want to trouble you with it, sweetheart," said Elihu. "It's nothing for you to worry about."

She smiled and watched him over her shoulder as she turned to walk away. "I'll just find them for you," she said.

Elihu had five brothers and four male cousins all living

on the ranch and working for him. Asa had been a different story. He had been a cousin, all right, but he had never worked a day in his life. He had robbed anything and everything he could for most of his life, and in the course of some of those robberies, he had killed men. He had returned to Hard Luck seeking a safe place to hang out. He had known that Elihu and his rough ranch hands ran just about everything in the county as well as the town of Hard Luck. So he had come back just to wait for his next opportunity to go out and get some money. The only honest thing he had ever done in his life was keep his deal with Sheriff Hardy. He didn't start any trouble in Hard Luck.

But trouble had come to him, and now he was dead. Elihu knew that Asa had brought the trouble on himself, knew that he had deserved what he had gotten, but that was just the beginning. He was a Hemp. He was a first cousin. And this stranger had dared to face him in the middle of Hemp country. And he had won. Elihu wished the man had caught up with Asa in some other town. Then it wouldn't matter so much. But right here in Hard Luck, it was a bad precedent. He did not want anyone thinking that anybody could take on the Hemps right in the middle of their home. Damn Asa, he thought. He's brought us trouble. Now we're going to have to kill this stranger, even though he doesn't deserve it. Asa was wanted for murder, and even so, the stranger gave him a chance. But we have to kill him. And the sooner the better.

Ezra Hemp was out riding the range at just that moment, so he did not make it to the meeting that Elihu had called. He was out with three of his cousins. They had a little job to do. There was a small ranch nestled in between the Hemp spread and that of Carl Doaks. It had good water, and Elihu wanted to add it to his own property in the worst way. He had told Ezra to take charge of the operation. The small place was owned by Merilee Hornbuckle and her brother Morton. They couldn't afford to hire any help, so they did all the work themselves. Elihu had made them an offer, one that he considered a little more than fair, but they had refused it. So he had told Ezra to cause them some little problems. Frustrate them. Annoy them. Run off some cattle. Start some small fires. Things like that. Convince them that they'd be better off selling the place. But don't hurt anyone. Elihu did not want anyone hurt. Not yet.

Ezra and his three cousins were sitting on their horses on a hilltop overlooking the Hornbuckle spread. They had stolen some cattle a couple of weeks earlier, and just the week before they had started a fire on the north pasture. The Hornbuckles seemed more determined than ever to hang onto their place. Ezra figured they had to do something a little more drastic to change the Hornbuckle minds. It was already dark. They could see a wisp of smoke rising from the chimney of the little log house, and there was light in the windows, probably from one lone lamp inside. There were four horses in a small corral behind the house.

"They couldn't get much work done without no horses," said Ezra's cousin Ferdie.

"I reckon not," Ezra agreed.

"You want we should go down there and run them off?" Ferdie asked.

"I don't suppose there'd be no harm in that," said Ezra. "Let's see if we can do it real quiet-like. You know, don't disturb them none. Elihu don't want no one hurt, do he? So let's just sneak down on that corral like little mouses, open the gate and kinda encourage them horses to wander off."

The three cousins all grinned wide grins. Ferdie's grin showed where two front teeth were missing.

"Come on," said Ezra. He started moving slowly down the hill, making no noise. At the bottom of the hill, he made a wide circle around the house, headed for the corral. When they got closer to the house, they could hear the sounds of a guitar being strummed. That's good, Ezra thought. It'll help cover up any little noise we might make.

They approached the corral, and Ezra reached out to lift the pole that served as a gate. The other end of the pole dropped and hit the ground with a thud. "Damn," said Ezra, dropping the end that he had hold of. It, too, clattered on the ground. The four horses in the corral whinnied and nickered and fidgeted around, stamping their feet.

"Whoa, there," said Ferdie. "Whoa up, little horsies. We don't want no trouble, so just keep quiet now."

The gate was wide open, so the four Hemp riders moved inside the corral. Slowly they worked the Hornbuckle horses toward the gate. One went out. The other three milled around inside the corral, dodging the Hemp horses. Their whinnying became louder. Ezra became frustrated. He took the coiled lariat off his saddle and slapped at the horses' rumps with it. "Go on," he said. "Get outa here. Get." He swatted one horse hard on the rear, and it nickered loud and long. The three cousins got the other horses out the gate just then, and the fourth one, the one Ezra was fussing with, turned to follow them. The Hemps trailed them out of the corral. The Hornbuckle horses, however, did not go far. If they just milled around the yard all night, they would be too easy to catch up in the morning.

"Damn it, boys," said Ezra, "we're going to have to make a little noise here to run these damn horses off. Let's chase them out of here."

He pulled out his six-gun and fired it in the air, yelling and screaming at the same time. Ferdie and the other two cousins did the same. They whooped and hollered and fired shots. The horse began to run. The front door of the log cabin flew open, and Morton Hornbuckle stepped out with a rifle in his hands.

"Hey," he shouted. He raised the rifle to his shoulder and drew a bead on one of the riders. He could not recognize any of them in the darkness, but he could damn sure see what they were doing. He squeezed the trigger, and

Ferdie felt the breeze of a bullet as it whizzed past his ear, way too close for comfort.

"Damn it," he shouted, and he turned in the saddle and fired a shot at Morton. Morton yelped and spun around, dropping his rifle on the ground. Merilee ran to the door and took in the situation quickly. She picked up the rifle and fired another shot, but the riders were already well away. She put the rifle down and knelt beside her brother.

"Morton," she said. "Morton, is it bad?"

"I don't know," he said. "I can't tell. It hurts. I never been shot before."

"We need to get you to a doctor," she said.

"With what," said Morton. "The nags are all gone."

"Oh, shit," said Merilee. "Well, come on. Can you stand up? Here. I'll help you."

With groans and moans, and with the help of his sister, Morton got to his feet and staggered into the house. Merilee got him to a chair and sat him down. Then she ran back outside for the rifle, brought it in, shut the door and barred it, and hurried back to her brother's side. She began examining the wound. The bullet had torn into his left shoulder up high. She pulled his shirt loose to get a better look.

"I'll do the best I can," she said, "but we'll have to get you into town some way."

"I don't see how," said Morton.

"Just don't you worry about it," she said. "I'll figure something out." She ran to put some water on the stove to boil, and she gathered up clean, white rags to use for bathing the wound and then for dressing it. She was glad to see that the bullet had gone all the way through, so she would not have to do any probing. As she daubed at the blood, Morton winced.

"Those goddamned Hemps," he said.

"Did you recognize any of them?" she asked.

"No, but you know damn well who they were. The goddamned Hemps. Couldn'ta been no one else but them."

3

Merilee patched up her brother as best she could. Then she made him more or less comfortable, and left the house to go after a doctor. She would have to go to Hard Luck. She looked around a bit for any one of their horses, but she never saw one of them. She couldn't wait around. She had to go. She started walking. Her feet were already hurting by the time she got to the road. She was about to turn onto the road to head for town when she noticed a rider back behind her, across the fence on Carl Doaks's property. She couldn't really make him out, for it was still dark, very early morning. She stood for a moment squinting toward the shadowy figure. She was having a hard time making a decision, for, she thought, it could be one of the Hemps. If so, he shouldn't be on Doaks's place, but then, they shouldn't have been on her place either. Still, he didn't seem to be making any mischief. She walked toward him.

Slocum was out early riding fence for Carl Doaks. It wasn't a tough job, but it was something he could do to at least make out like he was earning his keep. He glanced up and noticed the figure in the road. It was just a silhouette, but he could tell it was female. It didn't make any sense for a lone female to be out on the road on foot in the dark. He stopped his big Appaloosa and stared. She seemed to be staring at him. He touched the brim of his hat.

"Howdy, ma'am," he said. "You got troubles?"

"You're not Carl Doaks," she said. "Nor Sam Halter."

"No, ma'am. Slocum's my name. I just went to work for Carl yesterday."

"My brother's been shot, and our horses have all been run off," she said. "I have to get to town for a doctor."

"Come on over here," said Slocum. "You can ride double with me back to the ranch house. We'll saddle you up a horse, and I'll ride into town with you."

"Thanks," she said. She walked to the fence, and Slocum helped her climb over. He noticed that she was dressed like a cowhand, but underneath it all, she was a damn fine-looking woman. He thrilled a little at her touch as he helped her over the fence and then up onto his big stallion. Then he climbed on and started toward Doaks's ranch house.

"You say your brother's shot? Is it bad?"

"I don't know," she said. "The bullet went clean through. His left shoulder. High. I did the best I could for him, but I'd feel a lot better about it if a doctor had a look at it."

"Sure you would," said Slocum. "Say. Maybe we could hitch up a wagon and take your brother into town. It would be slower going in a wagon, but it would likely be faster than riding in for the doc and then riding back out to your place."

"That's a good idea," she said.

"You didn't tell me your name," Slocum said.

"Sorry," she said. "It's Merilee Hornbuckle. My brother's Morton. We own the place just next door."

"You got any help?" Slocum said. "What I mean is, your brother, is he there alone?"

"He's alone. There's just the two of us."

"Did this just happen last night?"

"Yeah."

"You know who done it?"

"Couldn't go to court with it," Merilee said, "but we know. It was them Hemps. Elihu, he's the leader of the clan, he's been trying to buy us out."

"That gives us something in common," said Slocum. "I figure they're after me as well."

"What have you got that they want?"

"Just me. I killed Asa Hemp, for the reward."

"They'll be after you, all right, but if you killed Asa Hemp, I'm sure glad to make your acquaintance."

When they arrived at Carl Doaks's house, no one else was around. Carl and Sam had both gone out the other direction that morning. Slocum hooked two horses to a wagon, got the bedclothes off his own bed and threw them in back, then wrote a hasty note to Carl Doaks telling him what he was up to. He turned his Appaloosa back in the corral and climbed up on the wagon with Merilee. They drove to Merilee's house and found Morton awake and moaning, and they helped him outside and into the wagon bed. Having made him as comfortable as possible, they started toward Hard Luck.

In town, Merilee showed Slocum the way to the doctor's house. He stopped the wagon there, and the two of them helped Morton to the front door, on which Merilee pounded loudly. They could hear the doctor's voice inside complaining loudly.

"Don't tear it down. I'm coming."

In another moment, he opened the door. When he saw Morton, his eyes opened wide.

"What is this, Merilee?" he said.

"He's been shot, Doc," she said.

"Well, come on. Get him inside."

They got Morton in and onto a table, where Doc started

his examination. He unwrapped the wound, cleaned it and wrapped it again. He looked up at Merilee. "Did you do this?" he asked.

"I had to," she said. "There wasn't no one else around."

"Well, you did a good job," said Doc. "You might even have saved his life."

"Is he going to be all right?"

"Why don't you leave him here with me for a couple of days," said Doc. "That way, I can keep a close eye on him. I'm sure he'll be just fine in a few days."

Morton stirred. "I don't need to—"

"Hush up," said Merilee. "We're going to do what Doc says. I'll be all right, and I want you to be all right, so that's the end of it."

Doc looked up at Slocum as if for the first time. "Who's this fella?" he asked.

"Sorry, Doc," said Merilee. "This is Slocum. He's working for Carl Doaks. He seen me and give me a hand."

Doc shook Slocum's hand. "Glad to meet you, Slocum," he said. "I'm Doc Grubbs."

"Howdy, Doc," said Slocum.

"We ain't been introduced either," said Morton, sticking up his good right hand to shake with Slocum. "I'm Morton Hornbuckle, and I thank you for what you done."

"It's all right, Morton," said Slocum. "Glad to be of help."

Slocum and Merilee left the doctor's place and walked back to the wagon. "I guess you've done had your breakfast," Merilee said, "but can I buy you a cup of coffee? I ain't had nothing to eat."

"You know a good place?" Slocum said.

She gestured ahead. "Just down the street there."

Slocum drove to the little café Merilee pointed out, and they went inside. While Merilee ate a hearty breakfast, Slocum drank coffee. When she finished her meal, she wanted one more cup of coffee, so Slocum had a refill and sat with her.

"So you got a reward for killing Asa?" she said.

"I ain't got it yet," he said. "Sheriff said I'd have to wait around for ten days."

"Ten days?"

"That's what he said."

"That'll give all the rest of the Hemps plenty of time to find out what happened and who did it. You're going to have to sleep with one eye opened."

"Yeah. That's what I figured. Doaks heard about it and offered his place for me to wait it out."

"So you'll have Doaks in trouble, too. You reckon all that trouble's worth the reward you're going to get? That is, if you live long enough to collect it."

"When you're broke, it is," Slocum said.

"Well," she said, pausing to sip her coffee, "I don't suppose Carl will mind. I think he'd love a chance to get at the Hemps. You just might be his chance. Me and Morton, we'll side you, too."

"I don't aim to get anybody else mixed up in my troubles," said Slocum.

"Don't worry about it," she said. "We've already all got our own troubles with the Hemps."

"I haven't heard Carl say anything about any trouble."

"That's on account of my place is closer to Hemp's than he is. If Hemp once gets my place, he'll be after Carl's next. Mark my words on that."

Slocum pondered Merilee's words. It looked like he was about to find himself right smack in the middle of a range war. He tried to weigh that against his two thousand dollars, and he asked himself the same question she had asked earlier. Was it worth it? He wasn't sure. Doaks was a good man, and Slocum did not like running out on a good man in trouble. But then, he had only Merilee's word that

Carl Doaks was in trouble. Then there was Merilee. She was a fine woman and unattached. She lived and worked on her ranch with just her brother. And she was in trouble. Her home had been attacked the night before by someone, and she and her brother both seemed convinced that it had been the Hemps. They had run off the horses and shot Morton. That was pretty serious. He decided that he would for sure wait out the ten days. Maybe something would happen in that time to convince him one way or the other. Stay or go.

"I've got a question for you," Slocum said. "I hope you won't take offense."

"Try me," Merilee said.

"How come a fine-looking woman like you ain't got a husband to help run that ranch of yours?"

Merilee smiled. "I guess that's a fair question," she said, "and thanks for the compliment."

"My pleasure."

"I had a husband. He was living here on the ranch with me and Morton. I married him too young. He really wasn't worth a shit. Lazy. He just wanted to lay around and let us do all the work for him. He'd take my money, when I had any, and get drunk in town. One day he asked me for some money, but I didn't have any. He got real mad and said that he was going to find Elihu Hemp and sell him the place. He saddled up a horse and took off. I never saw him alive again. Someone found him about halfway to town. His neck was broke. We figured he got himself throwed somehow. He never was much of a hand with horses."

"Oh," Slocum said. "I ain't sure what to say."

"Congratulations would be okay."

They were about to get up and leave when Sheriff Hardy came walking in. He walked straight to their table and sat down without waiting for an invitation. "What happened?" he said.

"What are you talking about?" said Merilee.

"You know damn well," said the sheriff. "You brought

your brother in here to Doc's all shot up. I want to know what happened."

"Why, Sheriff?" she said. "Do you mean to do something about it?"

"Just answer my question," said Hardy.

"She told me," said Slocum, "that someone showed up at her place last night after dark and run off their horses. Her brother come out of the house with a gun, and one of them shot him."

Hardy looked at Merilee. "Is that about it?" he said.

"That's it."

"Did you recognize any of them?"

"Not a one."

"Are you sure?"

"Hell, Hardy, it was dark. When I come out of the house, my brother was on the ground shot. I never got a real good look at them. But I know who they was and you do, too."

"If you didn't see them, then we don't know who they were," said the sheriff. "I want to come out to your place and have a look around."

"Suit yourself."

Slocum and Merilee were outside headed for the wagon, and Sheriff Hardy was going for his horse, when a big man with a drooping mustache stood on the sidewalk looking at them. "Hey," he said.

"You talking to me?" said Slocum.

"That's right," said the man. "Is your name Slocum?"

"I'm Slocum. Who're you?"

"The name's Eben Hemp. Asa was my cousin. I mean to kill you, so go for your gun."

"Go to hell," said Slocum. He turned his back on Eben Hemp and helped Merilee into the wagon. Several people on the street stopped to watch.

"Slocum," shouted Eben.

Slocum looked over his shoulder in time to see Eben's

gun coming out of the holster. He threw himself to one side and on the ground, as Eben's shot smashed into the side of the wagon. The horses snorted and fidgeted. Slocum's Colt came out fast and a shot rang out. The bullet smashed into Eben's chest. Eben looked surprised. He staggered back a few steps, looking down at the spreading red stain on his shirtfront. His right arm weakened and fell to his side, and the fingers of his right hand lost their grip. His revolver fell to the street. "Slocum," he said, "you—

Then he fell back straight as a board and did not move again. He was dead. Merilee looked at Slocum as he was getting back up to his feet. "You all right?" she asked.

"Good as new," he said, holstering his Colt.

"Well," she said, "that's two Hemps down."

Sheriff Hardy came riding up and stopped his horse near the body. He dismounted and stood for a moment looking down. "Eben Hemp," he said. "Slocum, can't you come into Hard Luck without killing a Hemp?"

"He came at me first," Slocum said.

A man came walking over from across the street. "That's right, Sheriff," he said. "Hemp there pulled his six-gun and fired first. This fellow didn't have no choice. Self-defense, pure and simple."

"All right," said Hardy. "Run down the street and fetch Elmo over here."

"Sure thing," said the man, and he turned to run for the undertaker. Hardy turned back toward Slocum and Merilee.

"I'm afraid that trip out to your place will have to wait. I got to ride out to Hemps's place and tell Elihu what happened here."

"Yeah," said Merilee. "First things first."

Slocum climbed up on the wagon seat and picked up the reins. He decided right then for sure that he was going to have to stick around and see this thing through. The Hemps were after him. There was no doubt about that. And he did not like looking over his shoulder. He would not run from this fight.

Hardy reached the Hemp spread before Slocum got to Doaks's place. He walked up to the door and knocked, and the door was opened by Elihu Hemp. "Hardy," said Hemp. "Come on in. What brings you out here?"

"It's business, Elihu," said the sheriff. "Not pleasure."

"Well, sit down and have a cup of coffee anyhow," Elihu said. Hardy took a chair as Elihu called over his shoulder, "Emilie, would you get the sheriff a cup of coffee?"

Emilie's voice came back from the kitchen. "Of course, Dear."

"Elihu," said Hardy, "someone raided the Hornbuckles last night."

"Oh?"

Emilie came out of the kitchen with a cup of coffee and handed it to the sheriff. He thanked her, and she left the room again. Hardy took a sip.

"Ran off their horses and shot young Morton."

"Kill him?" asked Elihu.

"No. He'll recover."

"If you're suggesting that I had anything to do with it—"

"I ain't suggesting nothing," said Hardy. "Of course, the Hornbuckles are sure that you did."

"Well, they're dead wrong," said Elihu. "That's all."

"That ain't the only thing."

"Well?"

"Eben's dead. His body's in town at Elmo's place."

Elihu's face turned white. "What happened?" he asked.

"He picked a fight with Slocum," said Hardy. "There were plenty of witnesses. It was self-defense."

4

Slocum dropped Merilee off at her ranch and drove the wagon back to Doaks's place. It was nearly noon, and Carl Doaks and Sam Halter were just riding up to the ranch house. They met Slocum near the barn. "Where you been?" said Halter, a grouch on his face.

"I guess you ain't been back to the house since this morning," said Slocum, looking at Doaks and ignoring Halter. "I left you a note."

"No," said Doaks. "I ain't seen it."

"I was out at the fence over yonder," said Slocum, "when Merilee Hornbuckle came walking up."

"Walking?" said Doaks.

"Yeah," said Slocum. "She told me some riders had come by her place last night and run off all their horses. Morton come out of the house with a rifle, and one of the riders shot him. I brought her over here and hitched up the wagon."

"Is Morton all right?" asked Doaks.

"I think he'll be all right. We left him at the doc's place in town."

"Did she recognize any of the riders?" Doaks asked.

"Nary a one," said Slocum.

31

"I bet we know who they are though," said Halter.

"Say," said Doaks, "lunch can wait. Let's all of us ride over there and help catch up their horses."

Slocum put the team away and saddled his Appaloosa. Then the three of them rode over to the Hornbuckle spread, leading an extra horse. They found Merilee in the house ready to fix herself something to eat. When she found out they had not eaten yet, she fixed enough for all four, and they had a hearty lunch. "No sense putting this off no longer," said Doaks. "Let's get to looking for them horses."

The four of them mounted up and rode off in different directions. Slocum caught up one horse right away. He brought it back to the corral and saw Doaks coming in with another. "This ain't going to be so tough," said Doaks.

"Not when you got horses to ride," Slocum said.

"Yeah."

"Here comes Halter with two more," said Slocum.

With four horses in the corral, they started to ride out again when they saw Merilee riding in. When she saw the four horses and the three cowhands, she kicked her mount into a run. Hurrying up to the corral, she stopped the horse. With a big smile on her face, she said, "You got them all."

"Glad to be of help," said Doaks.

"You want to climb down and set a spell?" she said.

"We got work to do," said Halter.

"It can wait," said Doaks. He swung down out of his saddle and the others did the same. "I was kind of wanting to have a little talk with you anyhow."

"You want to go in the house for some coffee?" said Merilee.

"Sounds good," said Doaks. They all followed Merilee into her house. It was small but neat and clean. Merilee indicated chairs around the table, and the men all sat down, while she brought cups and a coffeepot. She filled all the cups and sat down herself.

"What was you wanting to talk about, Carl?" she asked.

"I've thought about this before, Merilee," said Doaks. "Now with Morton laid up, it seems a good time to bring it up."

"I'm listening."

"Why don't we take down the fence between our two places and run our herds together. There's four of us here, and we ain't got so many cows between the two of us that we can't take care of them. My cows are all branded, and we can tell which mama the calves belong to. It seems to me there's a whole lot to be said for it, and now that you're working your whole spread alone, well, it just seems like an even better idea."

"You got three men," said Merilee. "I'm just one woman. You'd be doing most of the work, looks like."

"Still seems like a good idea," said Doaks.

"Who's the boss?" said Halter. "I ain't working for no woman."

"You're working for me, Sam," said Doaks. "Don't worry about it."

"Well," grumbled Halter, "I just wanted to make sure. That's all."

Merilee looked at Slocum. "Seems like a fine plan to me," he said.

She stuck her hand out toward Doaks across the table, and he took it in his and shook it. "It's a deal, Carl," she said.

Doaks stood up with a big grin on his face. "All right, boys," he said, "let's get to tearing down a fence."

Slocum took note of the way Doaks looked at Merilee and the satisfaction he saw in the man's face at the idea of tearing down the fence between their two ranges. He recalled the simple thrill he'd gotten from Merilee's touch that morning, and he decided that maybe he had set his sights in the wrong direction. Maybe Merilee was already sighted in on. He followed Doaks and Halter out of the house. Merilee came along behind them. They all mounted up and rode to the fence. They cut wire and roped and pulled down fence posts. They worked all afternoon. When they finally had it all down, they had to drag it all together in a pile. That much wire stretched out across the prairie could be dangerous for cattle. Working with gloves on, they rolled the wire up on the fence posts as best they could and piled the posts all up together. Finished at last, they mopped their brows and took long drinks of water from their canteens. The day was about done.

Elihu Hemp was trying to decide if he wanted a flat-out range war. He knew he could win it. Even if the Hornbuckles threw in with Doaks and Slocum, they would still be far outnumbered by his crew. He could ride over and wipe them out in one swift and merciless attack. His problem was Sheriff Hardy. Hardy was his man—almost. He had never pushed Hardy this far before, and he had no idea how the man would react. The evidence was all on the side of Slocum. He had killed two Hemps, but there had been witnesses, and each time, the Hemp had gone for his gun first. So now, if any of the Hemps were to go after Slocum, which of course they had to do, they would have to be very careful. They would have to make sure that it was a fair fight, or they would have to make sure that there were no witnesses. But a full-scale attack on the two small ranches would be far too obvious. He couldn't take a chance like that.

He called his brothers and cousins together for another meeting. When he laid out his dilemma to them, Micah Hemp stood up. "Elihu," he said, "I ain't never seen the man I can't outdraw. I'll take him. In front of witnesses."

"You can't draw first," said Elihu.

"I'll let him draw first," said Micah. "I don't give a damn."

"From what I've heard," said Elihu, "I don't think he will."

"I'll call him all kinds of yellow-eared coward," said Micah. "I'll make him go for his gun."

"You can try, Micah, but just remember what I said. We need witnesses, and he has to draw first."

"It's a cinch."

"Well, all right. You catch him in front of some witnesses, and you try it, but in case it don't work, we have to have another plan. We were harassing the Hornbuckles, but Ferdie like to messed us up on that when he went and shot young Morton."

"That couldn't be helped, Elihu," said Ezra. "Morton come out a shooting. Ferdie was just defending hisself."

"I don't think the law would call it self-defense if you was to shoot a man who was defending his own property from you," Elihu said. "In the future, we'll have to be a lot more careful. I blame you, Ezra. You shouldn't have gone so close to the house to bring Morton out. You should've found something to do other than run off the horses."

"Well, hell," said Ezra, looking down at the floor, "it sure did seem like a good idea."

"Think these things through," said Elihu. "Remember this. We've had a good thing going here with Hardy as sheriff, but we can't push Hardy too far. He'll look the other way, up to a point. But we don't want to get him on our bad side. Ezra, I want you and the boys to ride out again tonight, but all I want you to do is to get a good look at the situation. Find out where Slocum is staying. See where all the cattle is at. Make sure we ain't got no more to deal with than Slocum, Doaks, Halter and the girl. That's all. Don't do nothing else."

"What if Slocum comes up on us?" asked Ezra.

"I doubt if he will after dark as long as you keep away from the house."

"But what if he does?"

"Then kill him."

• • •

"Carl," said Slocum, "I don't like the idea of Merilee staying over there at her place all alone. Why don't you ride over there and spend the night with her?"

"I couldn't do that, Slocum," said Doaks. "I can't just go up to a gal and say I'm spending the night with you—all alone—the two of us."

"I guess I'll have to do it then," said Slocum, "but I won't do it like you said. I'll just slip up and bed down out by the corral where I can keep an eye on things."

"That's a good idea," Doaks said. "I'll feel better about it, too, if you do that."

Slocum rode up to the Hornbuckle corral as quietly as he could. It was well after dark, but there was a bright moon that night. At the corral, he unsaddled the Appaloosa, tossed the saddle on the top rail of the corral fence and turned his big horse into the corral with the four Hornbuckle horses. Then he unrolled his saddle roll on the ground just outside. One of the horses inside bumped into the Appaloosa, and the Appaloosa nipped at it. The horse made a loud snort and a nicker and ran around the corral. The front door of the house came open, and Merilee stepped out, rifle in hand.

"Who's there?" she shouted.

5

Slocum stepped toward the house and called out, "Don't shoot. It's just me."

"Slocum?" said Merilee.

"Yes, ma'am. I didn't mean to disturb you."

Merilee lowered the rifle and walked toward the corral. "Well," she said, "what are you doing here?"

"We, uh, talked it over back at Carl's house," Slocum said, "and we didn't none of us like the thought of you staying over here all by your lonesome. I volunteered to come over and sleep outside and kind of keep an eye out, you know."

"You were going to stand guard over me all night and never tell me?"

"Well, yeah, I guess that's about it."

"Did it ever occur to you that I might rest easier knowing that I was being watched over?"

"Well, no, I guess it never did. I just—"

"Oh, shut up, Slocum," said Merilee. "Pick your stuff up off the ground and come on in the house."

"I don't know if I ought—"

"Come on," she said, and her voice was insistent. Slocum rolled up the blanket and followed her into the house. He shut the door behind him, and Merilee walked over and barred it. Slocum felt a bit awkward. It was not that being alone with a beautiful woman bothered him. He was thinking about Carl Doaks and his feelings. He felt like an interloper or a rustler or something. Merilee walked over to a shelf on the wall and pulled off a bottle of bourbon. "How about a little drink before we turn in?" she said.

"Oh, no thank you, ma'am. I— Well, hell yes. That sounds like a right good idea to me. I'll sure join you in a short one."

Merilee brought the bottle and two glasses to the table, and she and Slocum both sat down. She poured the drinks. Slocum almost turned his down, but he quickly rethought it and took a modest sip. It would last longer this way, and he wouldn't be tempted to have another. He certainly did not want to get himself impaired in any way on this particular night. In the first place, he was there to insure Merilee's safety in case any of the Hemps came around again. In the second place, he wasn't at all sure just what she had in mind, but he wanted to be ready for whatever it might be.

"So you fellows were thinking the Hemps might come around again, and you didn't want me to get caught over here with my britches down, uh, so to speak," Merilee said.

"Well, yeah," said Slocum, taking another short sip of his whiskey. "That was the general idea."

"If they come around here, I'd have knocked at least one of them out of the saddle," she said.

"And maybe got shot for your trouble the way your brother did," said Slocum.

Merilee ignored that comment. "I ain't scared to stay here by myself," she said, and then after a pause, "but I'm glad you came. Thanks."

"Aw, don't think nothing about it," Slocum said. He took another sip and tried to keep his eyes off of her. When he glanced in her direction, though, he found her staring at him with big, brown eyes. He thought that her stare could melt a man right away. He looked back down at his whiskey glass. Carl Doaks is enamored of this woman, he told himself. The moments that followed were slow and awkward. At last both glasses were empty.

"I think it's about time we turned in," Merilee said. She stood up, and so did Slocum. She walked over toward her bed, and Slocum got his blanket roll and tossed it out on the floor on the far side of the room. He took off his gunbelt and hung it on a chair. Then he pulled off his boots and started to lie down on the blanket. Merilee said, "Slocum." He turned to see her pulling off her shirt. "Don't you think you'd sleep more comfortable if you undressed?" She dropped her shirt to reveal herself naked from the waist up. Her breasts stood out firm and luscious. Slocum stood frozen in place. She walked over to him and helped him out of his shirt. Then she took him by the hand and led him across the room to the bed.

Well, he thought, to hell with Carl Doaks and his hesitation. I didn't bring this on anyhow. He thought that he must have been wrong about Doaks and Merilee anyhow. They stood there facing each other and slipped out of their trousers. Slocum's rod had taken all of this nonsense it could handle, and it stood out firm of its own volition. Merilee looked down at it with pleasure.

"You don't know how long it's been," she said. She put her hands on his shoulders and pulled him close to her, looking up into his face. He leaned forward enough to kiss her firm on the mouth. Their lips parted and their tongues dueled for a moment. Slocum's hands slid down her back to grip her round, firm buttocks. His rod began to buck, and she could feel it bouncing against her, and she knew where it was longing to go. She broke away from the kiss and turned to crawl into the bed, pulling him after her by one of his arms. She did not have to pull hard. He willingly, anxiously, followed her. She lay on her back in the center of the bed, and Slocum moved in on top of her. Her legs were spread wide, and he moved in between them.

"Oh, baby," he said.

"I'll be your baby tonight," she said.

She took his cock in both of her hands and rubbed its head up and down the length of her slit. With each trip, he could feel her growing more and more ready, softer, wetter. At last she stopped, placing the head in just the right spot. Slocum thrust downward, driving his hungry rod deep into her waiting well.

"Ahh," she cried, hunching upward with her hips. "Oh, yes, yes, yes."

"Let's just do the same thing over again," said Ezra Hemp. "It ought to frustrate the hell out of that gal to have to chase her damn horses ever morning."

"I got in trouble the last time," said Ferdie. "Elihu said for us to stay clear of the house."

"Aw, hell," said Ezra, "we won't make no noise this time. Looky. The house is dark. We know that the gal's brother is in town at the doc's place. What can go wrong?"

"Them stubborn horses don't want to leave the corral," Ferdie said.

"All right," said Ezra. "Listen to me. What we'll do is we'll ride down there slow and easy. Two of you boys will lift the pole gate off and lean it real easy against the fence. Then we'll just ride into the corral, and each of us will take just one horse and lead it out real slow and quiet. We'll lead them off a good ways and then shoo them off."

Sam Halter could not go to sleep. He was thinking about Slocum and Merilee. Deep inside, he had a longing for Merilee himself, but he had never let on. He knew how Carl Doaks felt about the girl, and he did not want any trouble with Carl. He liked his job. Well, he had liked it well enough until Slocum came along. If anyone besides himself was going to get into Merilee's britches, he sure did not want it to be that goddamn Slocum. Carl was sound asleep when Sam crawled out of bed and slipped back into his clothes. Strapping on his six-gun and taking his Henry rifle, he sneaked out of the house as quietly as he could. Then he saddled up a horse and rode out toward the Hornbuckle spread.

The first thing that Sam noticed when he got to a spot on top of the hill near the Hornbuckle house was the Appaloosa in the corral. Slocum was there all right. He looked around for some sign of Slocum sleeping out on the ground, and he could find nothing. The son of a bitch was in the house with Merilee, sure enough, he said to himself. It was just as he suspected. The next thing he saw was the riders moving out of the woods and toward the corral. He hesitated but a couple of seconds. Then he slipped the Henry out of the scabbard, cranked a shell into the chamber and put the rifle to his shoulder.

The Hemp riders moved quietly to the corral. Two of them lifted the gate pole and leaned it against the fence. According to Ezra's plan, they started riding quietly into the corral, each one going for a horse. They had not planned on Slocum's Appaloosa. The big horse reared and squealed.

Inside the house, Slocum and Merilee were lying quietly side by side, enjoying the afterglow of their recent romp. Both of them heard the cry of the big Appaloosa. "The horses," said Merilee, but Slocum was already on his feet. Stark naked, he raced across the room to grab his Winchester. He worked the lever as he hurried on over to the door and tossed the bolt aside. He threw open the door and put the rifle to his shoulder. He could see the riders in the corral. Before he could fire, a shot rang out from somewhere off to his left. It was high, and it knocked the hat off of Ferdie's head.

"God damn," Ferdie shouted.

Forgetting their plans, the Hemp riders hurried out of the corral, bumping their horses into one another as they moved. Slocum could not recognize any of them, but their outlines were plain enough in the moonlight. He could see that one rider was already getting away. No matter. All he needed was one, and the other three were still trying to get control of their mounts and avoid running into one another. He took careful aim at the back of one of the riders, the one closest to him, and he squeezed the trigger. Just as he did, the rider's horse gave a frightened whinny and reared up high. While he was fighting to maintain control of his mount, the rider caught Slocum's bullet in the left cheek of his ass.

"Ah, shit," screamed Ezra Hemp. "I'm ass shot."

Even so, he managed to keep his seat and get the horse moving ahead. The three riders raced off behind the one who had first run away. Slocum thought about taking another shot, but he decided against it. He put down the rifle and moved to get his britches. He had just pulled them on when Sam Halter rode up in front of the house. Slocum met him at the door, barefoot and shirtless. Halter gave him an accusing look.

"Ride on over to the corral and make sure the horses are all in there," Slocum said. "Counting mine, there's five of them. And put the pole back across the gate."

Halter thought about arguing, accusing, saying something, but he did not. Instead he did as Slocum had told him to do. Then he rode back to the house. Slocum was still standing in the doorway. "They're all in there," Halter said.

"Good," said Slocum. "I'm glad you come over to check, Sam."

"Yeah," said Halter, "I come to check all right."

Slocum thought about trying to defend the lady's honor by saying something like he only slept in the house, and his blanket was on the floor, but he knew that it would show itself to be a big lie. Besides that, Merilee stepped up beside him just then wrapped in a sheet.

"Did you run them all off?" she said.

"They're gone," said Halter.

"Well, thanks to both of you," she said.

"Yeah. Sure," said Halter, and he turned his horse and rode away without another word.

Merilee looked at Slocum. "What's wrong with him?" she asked.

Slocum was thinking that Halter was just being loyal to his boss. He had no way of knowing about Halter's secret yearnings for Merilee. He gave a shrug. "I'm damned if I know," he said.

Back at Doaks's place, Carl Doaks woke up when Sam Halter came back into the house. He blinked his eyes in the darkness. He could see that Halter was dressed and carrying his weapons. "Sam?" he said.

"It's me," said Halter.

"Where you been?"

"Oh, I couldn't sleep," said Halter.

"Well? But where you been?"

Halter got a match and lit the lamp. "I just rode over to the Hornbuckle place. Thought I'd check on them."

"Find everything all right over there?" asked Doaks.

"I got there just as some riders was moving into their corral." Halter went for the coffeepot.

"What happened?" said Doaks, coming to his feet.

"I sent a shot after them. Knocked the hat off one's head. They took off after that, but Slocum shot one of them in the ass. They all four got away, though. None of the horses was lost."

"Well, hell, I reckon it's a good thing you rode over there," said Doaks. He pulled on his jeans and moved over to help Halter build the coffee. "Four of them, huh?" he said. "Could you recognize any of them?"

"No. I was too far off, and it was too dark. If I ever see that ass-shot one, though, I'll sure as hell know him."

Doaks laughed. "Yeah," he said. "I reckon."

Halter stoked up the fire, and Doaks put the pot on top of the stove. He got two cups and put them on the table. Then he went back to get the rest of his clothes on. "Sam?" he said.

"Yeah?"

"You reckon we had ought to report this to ole Hardy?"

"I don't know what good that'd do."

"You're right, of course. Then again, it wouldn't hurt nothing, would it?"

"Especially if we ever spot that ass-shot one again."

Both men laughed at that. Then Doaks said, "They'll most likely keep him under wraps for a spell."

"If they got any brains in their head they will," said Halter.

Doaks was fully dressed by now, and he sat down at the table as Halter poured coffee into the two cups. He lifted his cup and took a careful sip of the hot liquid.

"Ah," he said. "That hits the spot." Halter sat down across the table from him. "Sam," said Doaks, "do you reckon those damn Hemps will ever figure out that they can't drive us off our places?"

"They ain't really tried yet, Carl," said Halter. "They just been trying to get us frustrated. You and the Hornbuckles. Kid stuff. That's all. If they ever get serious about it, they'll come all at once meaning to kill us off. They could do it, too. One big attack. They could wipe us out."

"What's keeping them from it?"

"I ain't for sure," said Halter. "As worthless as ole Hardy is, maybe they think that he'll only look the other direction for so much. Maybe they're trying to keep him on their side."

"Yeah," said Doaks. "It would be a whole lot better for them if we was to decide to sell out to him rather than get killed off."

"Yeah."

They sat and sipped their coffee in silence for a moment. Then Doaks spoke up again.

"You reckon Slocum and Merilee are up and about yet? We ought to ride over there and get started on our workday."

"Carl?" said Halter.

"What?"

"There's something else you ought to know. Something I ain't told you."

"Well?"

"Slocum didn't sleep outside last night."

6

Slocum and Merilee had finished their breakfast and were up and outside at the corral saddling their horses when Carl Doaks and Sam Halter came riding up. Slocum noticed the sour faces on the two riders right away. "Morning, Boss," Slocum said. "Something wrong?"

"I heard you had a little trouble out here last night," said Doaks.

"Nothing we couldn't handle," Slocum said. "Besides, Sam was here to give us a hand."

"Yeah," said Doaks.

Slocum figured by the long face Doaks was wearing that Halter had said something to him about what he and Merilee had been up to the night before. He had suspected right from the beginning that Halter was a chicken shit, and now he was sure of it. It was one thing to disapprove of someone's behavior. It was another thing altogether to run telling tales like a schoolboy. He longed to punch Halter in the nose, but it really wasn't his place to say or do anything about the affair. If Doaks was pissed off about it, it was up to Doaks to say something.

"Good morning, Carl," said Merilee. Doaks grumbled some response. "Sam," said Merilee. Halter touched the

47

brim of his hat and nodded. She, too, noticed the peculiar behavior of the pair. Slocum finished tightening the cinch on his saddle, and Merilee did the same. When she was finished, he was already mounted up.

"So what are we up to this morning, Carl?" Slocum asked.

"I don't know," said Doaks. "I thought we'd just ride over here and see what you two had in mind."

"Well, if you ain't got anything else lined up for us," Slocum said, "we was thinking that we might ride out and see if our two herds is mixing together all right, and if they've got enough grass where they're at. See if they might ought to be moved somewhere."

"That's all right with me," said Doaks.

Over at the Hemp spread, old Elihu had called another meeting. He was hot under the collar. He had told Ezra to keep his distance from the Hornbuckles and from Doaks and Slocum, and here Ezra had come home whining with a bullet in his butt. They had called out the doc to patch Ezra's ass, and they had said that Ferdie had been shooting at a coyote, and Ezra had somehow gotten in the way. Ezra was humiliated at having his behind messed with, and of course, it was hurting him something fierce, but he managed to survive the ordeal. At the meeting he was stretched out on a couch in the big room with a hard pout on his face. Ezra stood behind a large desk facing the crowd of cowhands.

"I sent Ezra out to get some information for me last night," Elihu was saying. "Told him to keep out of trouble. He comes home with his ass end shot and no information. I don't know any more than I did, and I'm short one hand. I don't know what I have to do around here to get anything done right."

"I found out something," Ezra whined. "That Slocum is staying at the Hornbuckle place, and there's at least one more staying there with him."

"So who's at Doaks's place?" Elihu shouted.

"I don't know," said Ezra. "We never got over there. Maybe they're all at Hornbuckles."

"Maybe," said Ezra. "Maybe. That's all I get. Damn it. Well, nobody's going out tonight. We're going to all stay right here on the ranch and mind our business till I can think of another plan."

"You ain't giving up on Slocum, are you, Elihu?" said Ezra.

"No," Elihu snapped. "I ain't giving up. This here is his third day. He's got to wait around for ten days. Remember? We still got a whole week to kill him. I ain't giving up. He's killed two Hemps."

"And ass-shot another one," said Ezra. "Me. That might be the worst of what he's done."

"Oh, shut up," Elihu said.

"Elihu?" said cousin Ferdie.

"What is it?"

"I know a way we could get rid of Slocum and never even get our hands dirty."

"What are you talking about?"

"There's an old boy over to Rabbit Junction that would kill his own grandma for five hundred bucks, and he ain't connected to us in no way."

The room grew silent for a long moment. Elihu turned his back on the small crowd. He took a cigar from a box on his desk, grabbed a match and struck it. He took a while firing up his smoke, and then he turned back to face his crew. "The meeting's over," he said. "All of you get on out of here. Get back to work. Just remember what I said. No one goes out tonight."

"I can't get out," said Ezra. "I can't even get up."

"Couple of you boys grab Ezra up by his arms and walk him out of here."

Two of the Hemps took hold of Ezra and pulled him to his feet. He howled with the pain. "Yow. Wait a minute. I can't— Ow. Ow."

As Ezra was being dragged from the room yowling, Elihu called to Ferdie. "Wait up a minute," he said. Ferdie hung back till the room was emptied. Elihu glared hard at him. "Who is this ole boy you mentioned?"

"Over to Rabbit Junction?"

"Who else, damn it."

"Name of Gordie Glad," said Ferdie. "He kind of hangs out over there. He'll do the job for five hundred, like I said."

"It kind of goes against my grain somehow," said Elihu, "but we kind of got our backs to the wall. Go find him, but keep him away from here. Tell him you'll pay him when the job's done. But you'll pay him in Rabbit Junction. I don't want you seen with him anywhere around here. You got that?"

"Yes, sir. I got it good."

"And here's another thing. He's got to do it in front of witnesses. If Slocum's found off somewhere with a bullet in his back, you know who'll get the blame. He's got to do it in front of Doaks and Halter or that Hornbuckle gal or in town. I want plenty of witnesses who'll swear it wasn't none of us."

"Okay."

"Get going then."

"Right now?"

"Right now," said Elihu. "Get going."

"Elihu?"

"What?"

"Can I take someone with me?"

"You're going by yourself. Now get out of here."

Slocum and the others found the two herds of cattle mingling together with no problems. There were several new calves, but they were hanging close to their mothers. There would be no problem in keeping straight what belonged to whom. They rode around the herd a couple of times.

Slocum got the feeling that he should be watching over his shoulder, but he tried not to let it show. He just had a vague sort of feeling that he could be in danger from either Doaks or from Halter. Somehow, he felt like Halter was the one he should really be careful of, but he couldn't afford to write off Doaks either. After all, he had bedded down with the woman that Doaks thought of as his gal. He wondered if Doaks might try to kill him for that. Some men would. Halter was something else, though. He'd had the feeling right from the beginning that Halter would not need much of an excuse to back-shoot him. For whatever reason, Halter had just not liked Slocum from the first moment he laid eyes on him.

They rode around the herd a couple more times before they all got together again. Doaks glanced back at the grazing cattle, and then he said, "Grass is getting kind of short around here. We might ought to move them off. Somewhere over closer to your place, Merilee."

"That's all right with me," she said.

"All right then," said Doaks. "Let's get them going."

They yipped and swung their ropes, and the herd started to move slowly toward the Hornbuckle place. In a mile or so, Doaks rode up beside Merilee. "Carl," she said, "is something wrong with you? You been acting mighty peculiar this morning."

"Naw," he said. "It ain't nothing."

"It's something, Carl. I can tell. We been friends too long."

"Well, it seems you found yourself a better friend."

"What? What are you talking about?"

"It ain't no secret, Merilee. Sam seen you last night, and he told me all about it."

"Is that it? Is that what's bothering you?"

"Ain't none of my business," Doaks said.

"Carl," she said, "you— You got no business acting like

that. In all this time, you never give me no reason to believe that you ever thought about me like—well, like that."

"The time just never did seem right for it," Doaks said.

"Carl, listen—"

But Doaks slapped his coiled rope against his horse's flank and raced off to chase a cow that had wandered a little away from the rest of the herd. Merilee sat in her saddle puzzling. She'd had no idea. Well, now she knew, but she guessed it was too late. Slocum was a saddle bum. She knew that. She had only wanted a good time with him. And it had been a good time, but— If only she had known about Carl's feelings. He wouldn't want her now, not anymore, not now that she had been—used. And Slocum would ride on when the time came. She had no delusions about that. God damn that Carl Doaks, she said to herself. Why in hell did he not ever speak up? Why did he have to be so shy? He'd had plenty of time. Damn him.

It was late that night when Ferdie rode into Rabbit Junction. He had been half-afraid that he would run into Slocum or someone somewhere along the way, and it had gotten worse when the sun went down. He had watched all kinds of eerie shadows moving along the trail. Once or twice he had almost pulled his shooter, but he had managed to refrain from doing so. They were only shadows. And he heard coyotes and hoot owls and other creepy night things. They never bothered him when he was out with the boys, but out alone like this on a late night with that damned Slocum on the loose, well, that was a different matter entirely. When he finally saw the lights of Rabbit Junction up ahead, he had been mightily relieved. He had kicked his tired horse into a run, so anxious was he to get in among people again.

He tied his horse at the rail in front of the Owl Hoot Saloon. There was just room. He could hear the noises from inside, and he knew that the place was crowded even before he looked in through the batwing doors. When he stepped inside, he could see at least three poker games going, all the tables in the place filled with drinking men, mostly cowhands, and men shoulder to shoulder almost from one end of the bar to the other. He had wanted to be among men, but he would really have preferred not quite so damn many of them. About half would have been some better. He squinted till he found a spot at the bar he could squeeze into, and he moved on in. He slapped some money on the bar and waited. There were three bartenders at work, all of them busy, but one finally noticed him and came up.

"What can I do for you, mister?" the barkeep asked.

"Whiskey," said Ferdie.

The bartender reached for a glass and a bottle and poured the glass full. "You want a drink or the bottle?" he asked.

"Oh, just leave the bottle," Ferdie said, and he shoved his money toward the barkeep, who took it and moved on to serve another customer. Ferdie downed his drink and poured another. Then he began to search the crowd behind him by looking into the huge mirror behind the bar. Most of the faces were unfamiliar. He recognized a couple of cowhands, but he didn't know them all that well and didn't care to visit with them. He spotted the local sheriff sitting at a table back against the wall with some other men in suits, probably town officials, Ferdie thought, or maybe some big-shot local businessmen. Ferdie did not care for the sheriff. He'd had a run-in with him once before. He'd been given the choice of getting out of town or getting thrown into jail. Ferdie got out. Finally, he spotted Gordy Glad. The man was smack in the middle of a game of cards. It was no time to disturb him. Ferdie knew that much. Well, he downed his whiskey again and again refilled the glass, he would wait.

Casually, Ferdie kept his eye on Glad in the mirror, and

then he noticed Glad reach for a pot, and another man reach out and grabb his hands, stopping him. There was too much noise in the place for him to understand anything that was being said, but he could see in the mirror that hot words were being exchanged. The other man suddenly shoved back his chair and stood up, and Gordy Glad had a shooter in his hand almost by magic, and it blazed away. The one shot tore through the man's right shoulder, and the man staggered back and fell, but he was caught by someone sitting down behind him. Ferdie turned around to look directly at the scene of the action. He saw the sheriff making his move. Everyone got suddenly quiet. The sheriff was over at the card table in short time.

"You could have killed that man, Gordy," he said.

"Could have," said Glad, "but no one paid me."

"Let me have your gun."

"It was self-defense, Sheriff," said another man at the table. "Clear and plain."

The sheriff looked around, but everyone seemed to agree. "Well," he said, "a couple of you boys get this man over to the doc's place." Two men started to help the wounded man out, and the sheriff turned back to Glad. "Gordy," he said, "you're walking a fine line."

"Like they told you, Blatch," said Glad, "the man tried to kill me. I was only defending myself. You know I don't go around looking for trouble."

"It sure does seem to follow you, though."

Blatch, the sheriff, turned and walked back toward the table where his friends waited for him. Glad gathered up his winnings, and the game he had been playing broke up. A couple of other tables emptied. Suddenly there was plenty of room in the saloon, although there were still a bunch of customers in there. Glad downed a drink and headed for the bar. Ferdie stepped out almost in Glad's path.

"Gordy," he said, "can I buy you a drink?"

Glad stopped and looked at Ferdie with a curious squint. "Ferdie Hemp is it?" he said.

"Yeah. That's me." Ferdie held up his bottle.

"Sure," said Glad. "Let's go back to the table and sit down." He turned and led the way, Ferdie following along with his own glass and the bottle. Glad sat down. Then Ferdie sat. Glad shoved his glass toward Ferdie, and Ferdie poured it full. Then he refilled his own glass. He lifted it and held it toward Glad.

"Here's to you," he said.

"So what brings you over this way?" said Glad. "Old Elihu let you out on your own, did he?"

Ferdie leaned over toward Glad and spoke in a low voice. "Elihu sent me," he said. "He sent me to find you. He's got a business proposition for you."

7

Gordy Glad got quiet and almost solemn. He looked around till he spotted an empty table in a far corner of the room. Then he picked up his glass and the bottle and nodded toward the corner. "Let's go back yonder," he said. Ferdie picked up his glass and followed Glad to the far table. They sat down again, and Glad emptied his glass and poured a refill. He offered the bottle to Ferdie, who took it and poured himself another drink. "So tell me," said Glad. Ferdie leaned toward Glad conspiratorially and spoke in a low voice.

"There's an old boy over toward our place," he said. "Actually, he's staying at one or another of the small ranches nearby. Either at the Hornbuckles' or the Doaks place. We ain't right sure which one. Anyhow, this old boy come into town and right off killed one of our kin. Then a couple a days later, he killed another one. And he shot Ezra in the ass. Elihu wants him dead. The sooner the better. Only thing is, he don't want it to look like there's any connection to the Hemps at all. He wants it done in front of witnesses so they can see that it wasn't no Hemp that done it."

"He want to pay five hundred for the job?" said Glad.

"I told him that was your fee, and he sent me on over to find you."

"So all I got to do is find this man with witnesses around and kill him?"

"That's right."

"How come him to shoot your kin?"

"First off he went for Asa on account of Asa was wanted by the law. He went for the reward. Asa tried him, and Asa got killed."

"Asa was pretty fast, wasn't he?"

"He was that."

"What about the second one?"

"That was Eben," said Ferdie. "He tried to face Slocum down in Hard Luck on account of what Slocum had done to Asa, but Slocum beat him, too. Killed him dead."

"Did you say Slocum?" asked Glad.

"Yeah. That's right. That's the man's name. Slocum."

"I've heard of Slocum," said Glad. "This ain't no ordinary job. Slocum's fast. Some say there ain't none faster. Not even me. I can't take this job for no five hundred."

"Well, how much then?"

"A thousand," said Glad. "I'll kill him for a thousand."

"I don't know, Gordy," said Ferdie. "Elihu agreed to five hundred. I don't know if he'll go for a thousand."

"Well, you go on back and talk to him," said Glad. "Tell him it's a thousand or nothing. That's my offer. He can take it or leave it."

"Gordy?"

"Yeah?"

"I ain't never heard of this Slocum before. You sure he's that bad?"

"He's that bad, Ferdie. Believe me. He's that bad."

Ferdie got drunk and went on over to the hotel for a room. He was not about to start back to the ranch as late as it was. He would start back first thing in the morning. He wondered what Elihu would say to Glad's offer. He was a little surprised that Glad had heard of Slocum, but then, these gunfighters all seemed to know about one another.

Ferdie was just tickled that he had never tried to start anything with Slocum, if he was really that bad.

Over in the saloon, Gordie Glad thought about this new proposition. So Slocum had pissed off the Hemps. They could take him if they'd all go after him at once. They were a mean bunch. He knew that. There was some reason, though, that old Elihu did not want it known that he was behind this. He wanted Slocum taken in front of witnesses. Slocum. That was a bad charge. Glad was not at all sure that he could take Slocum in a fair fight. To get him in front of witnesses, he would have to make it a fair fight. The witnesses would defeat the purpose if Glad were to draw first.

He tried to figure a way to get Slocum. He could maybe have old Elihu get all the Hemps together and get some witnesses around them. Then he could kill Slocum by himself, and the witnesses would swear that the Hemps were all someplace else at the time of the killing. But then, if he were to just blast Slocum in the back, how would he establish the time of the killing? That part could be tricky. There had to be another way. Some way to kill Slocum and keep the Hemps' names clear. He could hire his own witnesses and take them along with him. It shouldn't cost him too much. They wouldn't have to do anything. Just go along for the ride and watch. If he got Slocum, then he would have the witnesses he needed to swear that it had been a fair fight. If Slocum should get lucky and kill him, well, they could just ride on home and leave him lying there. He would have to decide who to hire to ride along with him. A thousand dollars was a lot of money. Then again, he thought, perhaps he was worrying too much about all this. Perhaps old Elihu wouldn't pay the thousand after all. Then that would be the end of it. Slocum would remain Elihu's worry, not Glad's. He poured himself another drink and leaned back in his chair.

It was the morning of the fourth day of Slocum's wait. He was riding fence where the fence ran alongside the road into

Hard Luck. He found a stretch where the wire was hanging loose, so he stopped and dismounted. He dug into his saddlebags for a pair of pliers, a hammer and a pair of gloves. He stretched the wire as tight as he could and tacked it to a fence post. He put the gloves and the tools back into his saddlebags and was about to mount up, when he saw Sam Halter come riding in. He stood beside his horse and waited for Sam's approach. Soon Halter was there beside him.

"Howdy, Sam," Slocum said.

"Slocum," said Halter, swinging down out of his saddle and unbuckling his gunbelt, "I know I can't outshoot you." He rebuckled the belt and hung it on his saddle horn. Then he stepped away from his horse.

"What's wrong with you?" said Slocum. "I ain't aiming to shoot it out with you."

"Well," said Halter, "that's just in case."

"I don't know what the hell you're talking about."

"I don't like you, Slocum," said Halter. "I didn't like you from the beginning. I don't think we need you around here, and I think you're trouble. I come looking for you to tell you that I think you'd ought to ride off from here. You'd ought to get away and stay away."

"Carl ain't told me I'm not welcome," said Slocum.

"No, he ain't," said Halter, "and neither has Merilee, I reckon."

"Just what has Merilee got to do with this?"

"She's Carl's gal. At least she was till you come along."

"Carl never said anything about that," said Slocum, "and neither did Merilee."

"Well, I'm saying it."

"Maybe you ought to just mind your own business," said Slocum, turning to mount his Appaloosa. Halter stepped forward quickly, grabbing Slocum's shoulder, spinning him around and slugging him hard on the jaw. Slocum fell over backward on the ground. He rubbed his chin, looking up at Halter.

"I'm making it my business," said Halter.

Slocum stood up slowly, backing away from Halter as he undid his gunbelt. Then he did with it what Halter had done with his own. Stepping away from his horse, he braced himself for a fight. "All right," he said, "we're even now."

Halter came racing in, and Slocum sidestepped, popping Halter on the side of the head as he moved past. Halter staggered sideways. He regained his composure and turned to face Slocum square. He danced around Slocum in a circle, looking for a way in. Slocum suddenly stepped in and swung a right, but Halter blocked it and swung his own. Slocum ducked under it. Then, still crouched low, Slocum drove a fist into Halter's gut. Halter whuffed with the blow and bent over. Slocum banged him in the side of the head, and Halter went over, landing on his back.

"There ain't no need for this, Sam," Slocum said. "Now we've both been on the ground. Let's call it even and quit."

Halter got to his feet. He looked at Slocum with hatred in his eyes. "Hell no," he said, and he ducked and ran straight at Slocum, catching him around the middle and driving him back with the force of his weight and his movement, driving him against the barbed wire of the fence. Slocum yowled with the pain. He grabbed Halter's ears in both of his hands and twisted hard, rolling them both to the right till it was Halter's back against the fence. Now Halter screamed with the pain. He struggled trying to push Slocum away from him, trying to turn Slocum as Slocum had turned him, but it was no use. The more he struggled, the more the barbs cut into his back.

"Have you had enough, you bastard?" said Slocum.

"All right. All right."

Slocum turned Halter loose and stepped away. Halter winced with the pain. Slocum's back was hurting, too, but he knew that he had managed to cut Halter's even worse. Halter staggered over to his horse and reached for his gunbelt. "Don't try it," said Slocum. Halter hesitated, took the belt in his hand and strapped it back on around his waist. Then he mounted up and rode away. Slocum watched him go. Then he strapped on his own gunbelt and mounted up. He continued riding the fence. When he finally arrived at the far end, he saw Merilee just riding up to her house. As she was dismounting, she saw him, too.

"Slocum," she called out. "Come on over for some coffee."

Slocum turned his horse and rode down to the place where they had opened the fence for the cattle. He rode through onto the Hornbuckle spread and dismounted there in front of the house. Merilee was standing there waiting for him. "Come on in," she said.

"Thanks."

Slocum followed Merilee into the house and pulled out a chair. He sat down but did not lean back. Merilee put the coffee on, then turned to face Slocum. She noticed his shirt was dusty. "What have you been doing?" she said, walking over to brush the dust away from his shirt. Then she noticed the tears in the back of the shirt and the blood on his back. "What's happened?" she said.

"Oh, nothing much," he said. "I just had a little argument with Sam Halter. That's all."

"It looks to me like it was more than a little argument," she said. "Take that shirt off."

Slocum stood up and pulled off his shirt. It hurt some as it was peeled off his back. Merilee looked at the gashes. "My God, Slocum," she said. "What did that? It looks like someone took a bullwhip to you."

"It amounts to about the same thing," he said. "I got rolled on a barbed wire fence."

"Fighting with Halter?"

"Yeah, but you ought to see him. He got it worse."

"Sit back down," she said. "I'll get something to put on that."

Slocum turned the chair around and mounted it like a horse, leaning his arms on the chair back. Merilee returned to the table with a bowl of water and some clean rags. She started bathing the cuts, and Slocum winced. When she finished with what she was doing, she tossed the bloody water out the front door. Then she checked the coffee and found it ready. She poured two cups and set one on the table in front of Slocum. He lifted the cup and took a sip. Merilee started to rub some kind of salve on the cuts, and Slocum winced again. In another minute, she was done.

"That's all I can do for you for now," she said, "except I'll find some clean rags and wrap you up."

"Aw," he said, "there's no need for that."

"Yes, there is. It'll keep you from messing up the back of another shirt."

She had him all wrapped up in another few minutes, poured him another cup of coffee, and then said, "Do you have a clean shirt in your saddlebags?"

"No."

"Well, Morton's got some here. I'll fetch you one."

She brought out a clean shirt and helped him into it. "Just what was this fight all about?" she asked.

"Oh, Sam just never has liked me," Slocum said.

"That's it? He just walked up and punched you 'cause he never has liked you?"

"Just about."

"Well, if you don't want to tell me, I guess I can't make you."

"Merilee," said Slocum, "there's something I been meaning to ask you."

"All right," she said. "What is it?"

"How come you got the same last name as your brother if you was a married woman?"

She gave him a curious look. "That's a strange question. Is that it?"

"That's it."

"When I got rid of the husband, I got rid of the name. Satisfied?"

"Yeah. Merilee?"

"What?"

"Was you and Carl— Well, was you Carl's girl?"

"No," she said, rather coldly. "Why'd you ask that?"

"Oh, nothing. It's just that Carl's been acting a little strange, and then Sam said that you was."

"Is that what the fight was about?"

"Yeah. It was."

"Carl Doaks never said a word to me," she said. "Till yesterday. If he wanted me to be his gal, he was sure quiet about it for a good long time. The big oaf."

Ferdie Hemp reached the Hemp place late that night. He looked up Elihu first thing. "Well?" said Elihu. "Did you find him?"

"I found him all right," said Ferdie, "but he didn't take the job."

"Oh? Why not?"

"He said that Slocum's some kind of a gunfighter, and he's damn good. He said he wouldn't take on Slocum 'cept for a thousand dollars."

"A thousand?" Elihu roared.

"That's what he said. He said that he wasn't for sure he could take Slocum in a fair fight. Said it's going to be a rough job."

Elihu paced the floor for a bit. Then he sat down in his big chair and looked at Ferdie. "Likely he's right," he said. "Slocum took Asa, and he took Eben. Far as I can tell, both of them was fair fights. Asa and Eben were both good. All right, Ferdie. Go back and tell your man I'll pay it. I'll pay the thousand. And here." He opened a desk drawer and took out some bills. "Here's five hundred. You can give him that and tell him that he'll get the rest when the job's done."

8

Sam Halter was a mess when he got back to the Doaks house that evening. Carl Doaks was already there whipping up something for them to eat. As soon as Halter walked in, Doaks could see that he had been hurt. His shirt was ripped and bloody, and his face was bashed up. Halter walked in the house and found a chair by the table. He sat down heavy. Doaks stopped what he was doing and moved over to Halter's side.

"Sam," he said, "what the hell happened to you?"

"Aw, I got into it with Slocum," said Halter.

"Slocum?"

"Yeah."

"Well, what for?"

"Nothing, I guess. I just don't like the son of a bitch. That's all."

"Well, pull off that shirt," said Doaks. "I'll do what I can to patch you up." Doaks went for a pan of hot water and some rags while Halter stripped off his shirt. "Are you sure there wasn't more to it than that?" he said. "How'd the fight start?"

"I guess it was kind of mutual," said Halter. "Or, hell, I guess I started it. I said something, and then I took off my gunbelt. Slocum took off his, and we went at it. That's all."

"You ain't telling me everything, Sam," said Doaks, daubing on Halter's back. "Just what was it you said?"

"I don't really remember," Halter said. "I guess I said something about him sleeping over with your woman. He didn't take kindly to it."

"My woman?" said Doaks. "Merilee?"

"Who else?"

"Sam, that ain't none of your business. I ain't never said nothing to Merilee. I like her, but she ain't my woman. Never was. Slocum had no way of knowing how I feel about her. Hell, she don't even know. Well, she didn't till afterwards. I said something then. Shouldn't have. It was too late then."

"I knowed."

"I guess I opened my mouth to you when I should've kept it shut," said Doaks. "Anyhow, Slocum didn't know, and Merilee made her choice. You ought to apologize to Slocum for starting that fight."

"I'll eat shit first," said Halter.

"Ain't no need for that. But how're you two going to work together?"

"I don't know. I guess maybe I'll just move on."

"Ain't no need for that either. Tell you what. I'll just suggest to Slocum that he stay on over at the Hornbuckle place. Merilee's over there by herself right now, and she needs someone around. You won't have to see him all that much."

"You'd put him over there with her?" said Halter. "Deliberate?"

Doaks walked over to a shelf on the wall and got a bottle of whiskey. He walked back and slopped some on Halter's back. Halter jumped up out of the chair with a shriek. "God damn it, Carl, that hurt like hell. Can't you at least give a man a warning?"

"Sit down," said Doaks. "Now listen to me. What Slocum and Merilee does is none of my business, and it sure ain't none of yours. It's settled."

• • •

Slocum and Merilee took the wagon into Hard Luck and stopped at Doc Grubbs's place of business. They found Doc in and Morton sitting up.

"Morton," said Merilee, "how're you doing?"

"I'm good as ever," said Morton. "Damn, I'm glad you're here. I'm ready to go home."

Merilee looked at Doc.

"He ain't good as ever," said Doc, "but I think he's ready to go home. He's on the mend, and as long as he don't go out to do no hard work for a few more days, he'll be all right. Bring him in to see me in about three more days and let me check that wound."

Morton jumped up ready to go, and Slocum noticed that he winced a bit as he did. Slocum knew that Morton had taken a pretty bad shoulder wound, and he knew that Doc was right. There would be no work for Morton for a while longer. Merilee paid Doc for his work, and the three of them walked out of the office. "How about a bite to eat?" said Merilee.

"That sounds good," said Morton.

They left the wagon parked outside of Doc's place and walked over to the eatery. There weren't many people in because it was not the regular mealtime. "You just made it," said the man behind the counter. "We'll be closing up in a few minutes."

"We won't dawdle," said Merilee. "Just bring us each a mess of whatever you've got back there."

"Beef stew," said the man.

"That'll do."

They sat down, but they didn't have long to wait. The man brought out the bowls of beef stew right away. "Coffee?" he said.

"Three cups," said Merilee.

They ate without talking much, drank their coffee and paid for the meal. Then they started on their way back to the wagon. When they got to it, they saw a man sitting on the wagon seat. Slocum did not know the man, but there was a familiar look about him. He was almost sure that the man was a Hemp. They stopped on the board sidewalk a few feet away. Slocum noticed that the man wore two guns.

"Micah Hemp," said Merilee.

"What the hell are you doing on our wagon?" said Morton.

"I was just setting here waiting on you all," said Micah.

"I reckon you mean you were waiting on me," said Slocum.

"If you be Slocum," said Micah.

"I'm Slocum."

"Then I'm waiting here to kill you."

"There's no need for it," said Slocum.

"You've killed two Hemps," said Micah. "That's need enough and more."

"They both drew on me," said Slocum.

"I don't know about that, and I don't care. I'm fixing to climb down off of this here wagon. You can go for your gun anytime after I get down."

"I don't even know you," Slocum said as Micah hauled himself down from the wagon and strode to the middle of the sidewalk. "I ain't going to pull on you."

"Then I'll just kill you like a dog," said Micah.

"Merilee," said Slocum, "you and Morton get on out of the way."

"Slocum," said Merilee.

"Go on," he said.

Morton took Merilee by an arm, and they moved into the street, out of the line of fire. "Just so you know," said Micah, "I'm the fastest of all the Hemps. And I'm accurate, too. I'm fixing to kill you."

"I don't want to kill you," said Slocum, "but if there's nothing that will change your mind, go for it."

As Micah's right hand went for his gun, Slocum threw

himself against the front wall of Doc's building and pulled out his Colt at the same time. Micah shot first, but his shot went wide. Slocum fired. His bullet tore into Micah's right arm just above the elbow. Micah roared with pain. Then he went for his left-hand gun. Slocum fired again. This time his slug ripped into Micah's left arm, entering just above the wrist and tearing out through the forearm below the elbow. Micah roared again. Then he stood there helpless, both arms dangling.

"You'll find Doc in his office," Slocum said. "Get patched up, and then go home and tell the rest what happened here. If you're the best the Hemps have got, like you said, then the rest had better let me be. Tell them I won't be so careful next time."

Slocum opened the door to Doc's office and stepped aside. Micah walked in groaning. Slocum shut the door and moved to the wagon. Merilee walked over, and Slocum helped her up.

"That was the goddamndest thing I ever saw," said Morton. "That was some shooting."

Slocum ignored Morton and climbed up to sit beside Merilee. He took up the reins. Morton got onto the seat, his eyes still wide with admiration. Slocum was about to flick the reins when he saw Sheriff Hardy coming at a run.

"He's in Doc's office," Slocum said. "I just shot him up some is all."

"Who?" said Hardy.

"It was Micah Hemp," said Morton. "You should have seen it. He went for his gun first, and Slocum drilled his arm. Then he went for his left-hand gun, and Slocum drilled his left arm. He's crippled up for sure."

"Is that how it happened, Merilee?" said Hardy.

"Just exactly," she said.

"I'm getting kind of tired of this," said Hardy.

"Then have a talk with the Hemps," said Slocum. "I'm tired of it myself. Tell them to lay off of me. I told that

Micah already, but I'll tell it to you, too. You can pass it along to rest of the Hemps. Next time I won't be so careful."

"I'll tell them," said Hardy. Then he opened the door to Doc's office and went inside. Slocum flicked the reins and the wagon started with a lurch.

Ferdie made it back to Rabbit Junction, but it was late again. He wished, if he was going to have to ride back and forth like that, that Elihu would send him out earlier in the day. He went into the saloon, but he did not find Gordy Glad. He asked for him, but no one could or would tell him anything. He had a couple of drinks and headed for the hotel.

He was up early the next morning, and he dressed and headed for an eating place. Inside he ordered eggs and ham, biscuits and gravy and coffee. It was the morning of Slocum's fifth day. Ferdie knew that. All the Hemps were counting the days. He finished his breakfast and was slurping down another cup of coffee, when Gordy Glad walked in. He waved Glad over to his table. Glad sat down across from Ferdie. When he'd ordered his breakfast and had a cup of coffee, Ferdie spoke up.

"You got a deal," he said.

Glad looked around to make sure no one was listening. "For a thousand?" he said.

"That's right," said Ferdie. "I got half of it right here for you. You'll get the rest when it's done with."

"That's all right with me," said Glad.

"When will you do it?"

"I ain't sure," said Glad. "I'll ride over to Hard Luck this morning. I'll have to locate the man and watch him for a day or two. Figure out his habits. Then I'll decide."

"Well, when it's done with, you just ride back over here to Rabbit Junction. I'll know when it's over with, and I'll ride back over here to pay you off. Elihu don't want no one to see us together."

He took out the five hundred that Elihu had given him

and slid it across the table. Glad palmed it and tucked it in his pocket. "I'll be seeing you in a few days," he said.

Slocum slept the night back over at the Hornbuckles' house. Carl Doaks had told him it would be best because Merilee was alone there. Slocum said that they had brought Morton home, but he was not yet in any shape to do any work.

"Or any fighting?" said Doaks.

"That, too," Slocum said. So he had agreed and had ridden back to tell the Hornbuckles. They had a small two-room house, with the second room being Merilee's bedroom. Morton's bed was in the main room. Slocum had rolled out his blankets on the floor of the main room. It wouldn't be as snug as his first night there, but that was probably all for the best. He had slept well enough. They were all up early for breakfast, and Merilee fixed them a fine one. They finished their coffee, and Slocum got up and went for his hat. Morton did, too.

"What are you doing?" Slocum said.

"I thought I'd just ride out with you," said Morton.

"Doc said for you to rest up for a few more days," said Slocum. "I think you'd best stay right here."

"Aw, hell," said Morton. "I'm just fine."

"Morton," said Merilee, "you listen to Slocum."

"Aw, Sis—"

"Merilee," said Slocum, "there ain't that much to do out there today. Why don't you stay here and ride herd on your brother?"

"That sounds like a great idea, Slocum," she said. "Thanks."

Morton slapped his hat back on the rack with a serious pout on his face. Then he stomped back over to his bed and threw himself down on it, folding his arms over his chest. Slocum folded his blankets up and set them aside. He strapped on his Colt, then picked up his saddle and his Winchester and walked out the door.

He went to the corral and saddled up the big Appaloosa. Then he started riding. He was going out to check the herd. He had already checked the entire fence line and mended the fence where it was needed. This day his intention was to see if there were any calves that needed branding. He hoped to run into Carl Doaks out there. He did not particularly want to see Sam Halter, but if he did, he would just deal with that when it came up. He found the herd grazing contentedly not far away. Sure enough, Doaks was there already. Slocum rode up to him.

"Morning, Carl," he said.

"Slocum," said Doaks. "How's Morton doing?"

"We had to fight him to make him stay home," said Slocum.

"Well, that's good," said Doaks.

"I thought I'd check the calves today," Slocum said.

"I've already looked them over," said Doaks. "The little ones are still hanging close to their mamas. I don't think there's any branding called for yet. You can check them for yourself though, if you want to."

"No, I'll trust you on that."

"Well, I think I'll get back to the ranch house," said Doaks. "I need to hook up the wagon and go in for some supplies."

"You need any help?"

"No. I'll manage all right. Sam's got some chores lined up around here. We'll see you later."

Slocum decided to go back to the house and check the corral and the barn. He knew that there was some work that could be done there. Everything else seemed to be under control. It was a slow time around the ranch, a time for tending to chores that had been let go. He would find those things and take care of them. He had five days left. He was getting anxious for his money.

9

Slocum was riding up to the corral at the Hornbuckle place when a shot rang out and a bullet smacked into the top rail of the corral fence. Slocum threw himself out of the saddle and onto the ground, pulling out his Colt as he landed. He looked around for some sign of where the shot had come from. There was a patch of woods over on the Doaks side of the fence, and on farther to his right there were some low, rolling hills. But from the angle the shot had struck the fence, it could not have come from the hills. It had to have come from the woods. A second shot sounded, and the bullet kicked up dust not far from where Slocum was settled. They were rifle shots, he could tell. He was suddenly afraid for his horse. A shot could easily strike the big Appaloosa. He looked around till he found a pebble, and he picked it up and tossed it at the animal's rump. The stallion jumped, and Slocum said, "Go on. Get out of here." It trotted away some distance to relative safety.

Now Slocum concentrated his attention on the woods, but he could not just lie there waiting. Whoever the shooter was, he was bound to get in a better shot sooner or later. Slocum thought about scooting under the corral fence, but there were horses in there that were already in some danger from the rifle shots. He looked toward the house. With a little luck, he could make a zigzag run to it and get himself behind a corner. Another shot kicked up dust nearby, and Slocum sprang to his feet and ran like hell toward the house. There was a shot while he was running, but it, too, missed him. Reaching the house, he flung himself around the nearest corner. He heard the door open.

"What's that shooting?" called Morton.

"Get back inside and keep the door shut," Slocum yelled.

He heard the door shut. He still had not spotted the shooter. Then he heard answering rifle shots coming from the house. Morton or Merilee, one of them, was shooting through a window toward the woods. Then, at last, he saw a movement in the woods. He raised his Colt, but he knew instantly that it was too long a shot for that weapon. He could tell that the movement was a man running, and soon he could hear the sound of a horse running away. The rifle shots from the house had done the trick and driven off the ambusher. Slocum holstered his Colt and walked to the front door. He opened it and stepped inside, and he saw Merilee with a rifle at the window. Morton was standing close behind her.

"Well, you ran him off," said Slocum.

"Who was it?" Merilee asked.

"I never saw him," said Slocum.

"We know who it was," said Morton. "It was one of the Hemps. Couldn't be no one else."

"You might be right," said Slocum.

"Course I am."

"Any sense in chasing after him?" Merilee asked.

Slocum shook his head. "He's long gone," he said.

"Those sorry bastards," said Morton.

"You might as well sit down and have a cup of coffee then," Merilee said. "I just made some fresh."

"Thanks." Slocum sat in a chair at the table. Morton

moved over to join him, and Merilee poured three cups of coffee. Then she sat down with them.

"So what are we going to do about the Hemps?" said Morton.

"I'm damned if I know," Slocum said. "Hell, I've done killed two of them. But I ain't sure that was a Hemp."

"What do you mean?" Morton said.

"They've all come at me face to face. I think they've got some pride about that. If this one was a Hemp, he's the first one to try bushwhacking me. On top of that, he wasn't too good a shot."

"They can't all be prideful," said Morton. "Maybe you've thinned out the ranks till you smoked out the cowards."

"Maybe," said Slocum, "but I can't quite see it that way."

In Rabbit Junction, Gordy Glad was all ready to head for Hard Luck. He was ready except for one thing. His horse was outside, saddled with a blanket roll tied on behind the saddle, and saddlebags with some provisions strapped on. Glad himself was dressed with two six-guns strapped on and a Henry rifle in his hand. His hat was on his head. But he was still in the saloon having a drink. One of the saloon gals, Red-haired Ruby, was standing at the far end of the bar looking bored as hell. Glad tossed down his drink and strolled down to stand beside her. She gave him a look of interest.

"You want to buy me a drink?" she said.

"Nope."

"You want to go upstairs?"

"You got it right that time," he said.

She turned and headed for the stairs with Glad walking in her footsteps. They went up the stairs to a hallway lined with rooms, and Ruby stopped at the second door. She opened it and stepped inside. Glad followed her and closed the door. She was headed for the bed, but he reached out and took hold of her by the arm, turning her to face him. She looked surprised. He pulled her to him, then turned them both around, pressing her back against the door. He reached down and felt under her skirt to see if she was encumbered there, but she wasn't. He dug a finger into her slit and found it wet and waiting. He brought his hand up to his face and sucked the juices off of his finger. She smiled at him. Then he reached with both hands to unfasten his britches underneath his gunbelt, and he let them drop to around his knees. Then taking hold of his hard and throbbing rod, he rammed it home. She gasped. With his six-guns still strapped on around his waist, with his suit coat still on and his hat on his head, he began humping her fast and furious, banging her against the door.

"Oh, oh, oh," she cried.

"Uh, uh, uh," he moaned as he jabbed his tool in and out, sloshing, thumping against the door, moaning and groaning. "I'm fixing to come in you," he snarled.

"Do it," she said. "Do it."

And he did, sending forth into her depths a torrent of hot juices. Spent at last, he hauled himself out. "Get me a towel," he said, and she moved away from the door to a small table on one side of the room. She brought him a towel, and he wiped himself clean. Then he tossed the towel aside, reached down for his britches, pulled them up and fastened them. He reached in a pocket for some money and handed it to her. Then he opened the door and walked out. Red-haired Ruby stood, as dressed as ever she had been, money in hand and alone in the room. Glad walked down the stairs, through the bar and out into the street. He mounted his black mare and turned her head toward Hard Luck. He had a job of work to do.

Carl Doaks was working on his corral. Some of the fencing needed mending, and he had been putting it off because other things were more pressing. This was a good time for it, though, and so he was tossing off broken or rotted pieces of fencing, crosspieces as well as fence posts. He just about had the whole thing torn down, but he had the new pieces stacked nearby and ready to go. He wondered where Sam Halter had gotten to. He thought that he could sure use some help here. Oh, well, Sam had likely found some other job that needed attention. He was a good hand. Doaks was grateful that he never had to worry about Halter, never had to tell him what to do. Halter was a good hand who always seemed to know what needed to be done, and usually he was doing it even before Doaks had thought about it. So Doaks kind of longed for Halter's help on the corral, but then he figured Halter was doing something else just as needful. Besides, the corral wasn't all that tough a job. He could handle it all right by himself.

He wondered what Slocum was doing over at the Hornbuckles' spread. He was glad they had brought Morton home, because that would make it much more difficult for Slocum to find time with Merilee alone. They wouldn't do it in front of Morton. Surely not. He wondered if Morton even knew what the two of them had been up to. Would he give a shit? Would he want to run Slocum off, or kill him? If it was my sister, Doaks thought, by God, I would. Finally he told himself to stop dwelling on such thoughts. He recalled what he had said to Halter. It was none of his business. He had kept quiet for too damn long, so he reckoned that he got what he deserved.

He lifted a fence post to drop it in place in the hole he had removed the old one from, and as he let it down, he heard the sound of approaching hooves. He looked up to see Sam Halter riding in. Halter rode up casually and dismounted close to where Doaks was working.

"Could you use some help there?" he asked.

"Sure thing," said Doaks.

"I just been out checking that north fence," said Halter. "Found one place that needed some mending."

"You take care of it, did you?" said Doaks.

"It didn't take long," said Halter. "Where do you want me?"

"Let's sit down and take a smoke first," said Doaks. "I need a break."

"Okay."

They moved to where Doaks had cut down some trees long before. The stumps were still standing, and they made good seats. Doaks took the makings out of his shirt pocket and handed them to Halter, who rolled himself a smoke in no time and handed them back. While Doaks busied himself with rolling one, Halter took out a match and lit his. Doaks licked the paper and finished off his cigarette, then stuck it between his lips. He tucked the makings back in his pocket and took out a match. As Doaks let out his first lungful of good-tasting tobacco smoke, Halter asked him, "Did you see Slocum anywhere today?"

"Saw him early this morning over by the herd," said Doaks. "Why?"

"Nothing. Just curious. We are all working the same herd."

"Yeah. It just don't need much tending right now."

"Grass is good. They got plenty of water. I ain't seen no wolves around for a spell."

"Yeah," said Doaks. "Even the Hemps has been pretty quiet lately."

"That's got me a little bit worried," Halter said. "Slocum's killed two of them and shot up two more. I can't see them giving up that easy."

"They want the Hornbuckle place, too," said Doaks. "I don't see them giving up on that either."

"Might be they're trying to lull us into relaxing. Forgetting about them. I say we stay on our guard at all times."

"I agree with you on that, Sam," said Doaks. "We'll check the herd at least twice a day, and it won't hurt anything if we sneak a look at the Hornbuckle house a couple times a day, too."

"Slocum's supposed to be watching that, ain't he?"

"He can't be just sitting there all the time. We'll watch it, too. Right now, let's get to that corral."

Morton Hornbuckle was up and moving around the house. Merilee kept her eye on him and fussed at him if it seemed to her he was doing too much, but he told her he was just exercising to loosen up his shoulder and get some strength back into it. He would fetch his own coffee, pouring it for himself. He helped her wash the dishes. He even carried in firewood. But anytime he started to look like he was about to saddle up a horse, she stopped him. "It ain't time for that yet," she said. Then he would back off and piddle around the house at some other little chores, grumbling some under his breath. Slocum took note of what was going on and kept well out of it. It was good, he thought, that the boy was trying to get back in shape and wanting to do his part. It was also good, though, that his sister was keeping a rein on him. He'd had a bad shoulder wound.

Late that evening, Ferdie Hemp rode back onto the Hemp ranch. Elihu was sitting on his front porch smoking a cigar and drinking whiskey. When he saw Ferdie ride up, he yelled at him to put up his horse and then come on over to the porch. In a few more minutes, Ferdie was there. Elihu offered him a cigar and a glass of whiskey, and Ferdie happily accepted both. Elihu waited till Ferdie was contentedly puffing on the cigar and sipping the whiskey before bringing up business.

"Did you conclude our business this trip?" he asked.

"I sure did," said Ferdie. "The man had ought to be riding into Hard Luck tonight."

"Did you see him leave?"

"Nope. I didn't want no one to see us together too much, so I left ahead of him, but he told me he was leaving this morning, and I took his word for it."

"Did he agree to my terms?"

"Ever' one of them. I told him he's got to have witnesses, and he agreed to that. And I told him that when he's done it, he's got to go on back to Rabbit Junction. Soon as I hear the deed's been done, I'll go on over there again and pay him off. I give him half the money already."

"That's satisfactory," said Elihu. But silently he wished that there had been some other way. It just didn't seem right that the Hemps should have to hire their killing done.

A little later that same evening, Gordy Glad rode into Hard Luck. He found the stable first thing and stopped by to put up his horse. Then, shouldering his saddlebags and his blanket roll and taking his Henry rifle in his hand, he strolled down the street to the nearest hotel. He went inside and paid for a room. He took his stuff upstairs and stashed it, then walked out again, headed for the saloon. It was still busy in the Hard Luck Saloon as Glad bellied up to the bar, but the barkeep was there pretty quick to tend to his needs.

"What can I do for you?" he said.

"A bottle of whiskey and a glass," said Glad.

The barkeep turned away, but he was back just as fast. He put the glass on the counter and poured a drink, then set the bottle down beside it. Glad paid him, but before the barkeep turned away, Glad said, "Have you seen a man in here called Slocum?"

"Slocum? Yeah, but not for a couple of days. I hear he's working out at the Hornbuckle ranch just outside of town."

"He ain't here now, huh?"

"No. Like I said, he ain't been here for a couple days. Maybe it was more than that. I can't be sure."

"If he comes in while I'm here, point him out to me," said Glad. "If he comes in anytime, let me know."

"How'll I find you?"

"I'm staying over at the hotel. My name's Glad. It's important that I find him. I got business with him."

Glad had taken the first step toward insuring that the Hemps would not be associated with the killing of Slocum. He had come into town a stranger and had announced to everyone in the bar that he was looking for Slocum. Even if he killed Slocum out of town and alone, he figured that he would be the first suspect now. It would be seen as one gunfighter killing another gunfighter in order to build up his reputation. He would make even more noise the next day.

10

Gordy Glad was having breakfast in an eating place in Hard Luck on the morning of Slocum's fifth day of waiting. He had finished eating and was having one more cup of coffee when the door opened and a man came in hacking and coughing. He shut the door and found himself a place at a table not far from where Glad was seated. His coughing fit grew worse, and it almost sickened Glad. He started to get up and leave, but a glance at the man caused him to hesitate. The wretch looked as if he had slept in the same clothes for a month or more. He needed a bath and a shave. When his fit finally subsided, he pulled some coins out of his pocket and counted them on the table. The waiter finally walked over to the table, the disgust on his face not disguised at all.

"What do you want, Jackson?" he said.

"Is this enough for some fried taters and some coffee?" Jackson said, pushing the coins toward the man. The waiter picked up the money and looked at it.

"It'll do," he said. He walked away with the money.

Glad figured this Jackson to be a hard luck case, probably a heavy drinker. He might be useful. He stayed and took one more cup of coffee, watching Jackson out of the

corner of his eye. When Jackson got his coffee and potatoes, he took one swig of coffee and started to hack again.
Glad wondered if he would die right then and there, but the
fit subsided, and Jackson started to eat. He got down most
of the potatoes before he had another attack. Glad waited
through two more cups of coffee, until Jackson was finally
finished and got up to leave. When Jackson had gone out
the door, Glad got up, paid for his breakfast and left. Outside, he looked up and down the street. He did not see Jackson at first. He heard him hacking. Then he saw him
leaning against a wall between two buildings. He thought
again that the man might drop over dead right there, but he
did not. He spat great gobs of nastiness onto the ground
and finally came out of the nook and started walking along
the board sidewalk. Glad followed him casually until Jackson paused at the door of the Hard Luck Saloon. He stood
there looking longingly through the door. It was way too
early in the day for a drink, Glad thought. He had been
right about the man. He was a drunk. Glad was a little surprised that he had spent his last few cents on food and coffee, but then it was probably not enough for a drink, and he
must have been starving. Then Glad saw Jackson make a
feeble gesture toward someone inside. He walked closer

"Brace," said Jackson, his voice wheedling, "I need a
drink. I ain't got—"

"No credit," boomed Brace's voice from inside the saloon.

Jackson turned away, but he did not leave. He looked
around as if he were hoping for someone to come up that
he could put the bum on. It was unlikely so early in the
morning. Glad strolled on down to where Jackson lurked
outside the saloon.

"Good morning, friend," he said.

Jackson looked at Glad with surprise, almost with fear.

"Uh, do I know you?" he said.

"Not yet. Can I buy you a drink?"

A look of profound relief spread over Jackson's face. He smiled. "Yes, sir," he said. "You sure can."

They walked inside, and Brace, the barkeep, turned on Jackson with a mean look. "Jackson," he said, "I told you—"

"He's with me," said Glad. "Bring him a bottle and a glass. Do you have any coffee?"

"Sure."

"Bring me a cup of coffee."

Glad and Jackson took seats at a table a fair distance away from the bar. Brace brought the drinks, and Glad paid for them. Jackson had a small coughing fit, but as soon as it was done, he poured himself a drink and tossed it down all at once.

"Ah," he said, "that's some better." He poured another and then looked up at Glad. "Mister, how come you to be so kind to me, a stranger?"

"I've got a job for you," said Jackson. "I'll keep you in whiskey. All you can drink."

"What do I have to do?"

"Just stay close to me wherever I go. Keep your eyes on me. That's all."

"I . . . I ain't no good bodyguard, mister," Jackson said. "If something happens, I won't be able to do nothing about it. I—"

"I don't need a bodyguard. I don't want you to do anything except watch."

Jackson squinted his eyes at Glad. He was curious. He did not understand. He did want the whiskey.

"Look," said Glad, "I've got a job to do, and when I do it, I want a witness who can swear that it was me did the job. Me and no one else. That's all I want from you. Witnessing. You think you can handle that?"

Jackson tossed down another drink. "Sure," he said. "Yeah. I can do that."

"All right then. We got a deal. When the time comes, my name's Glad. Gordy Glad. Remember it."

•   •   •

Morton Hornbuckle was out in the yard alone. Slocum and Merilee had both ridden out that morning to check the herd. Slocum had told Merilee that anything Morton might try to do on this day, short of go riding, was probably going to be good for him, so she did not need to keep watching him. She was relieved to hear that. She was beginning to get cabin fever. Morton was looking around for something he might be able to do. He went to the woodpile and picked up the ax, but it hurt his shoulder, so he put it back down. Finally, he rolled himself a smoke and lit it. He was standing in the middle of the yard looking around aimlessly while he puffed, when Carl Doaks came riding up.

"Morning, Morton," said Doaks.

"Morning, Carl," said Morton. "Climb on down."

"Thanks." Doaks swung down out of the saddle and let the reins trail on the ground. "How's the shoulder coming?"

"Aw, I guess it's getting better, but I can't hardly do nothing around here worthwhile. I'm feeling awful useless."

"A gunshot wound like that takes time to heal," said Doaks. "Feel lucky it didn't hit you a bit lower."

"Yeah," said Morton. "I know. What brings you around here? Merilee and Slocum rode out to the herd this morning."

"I know. I saw them going. I just thought I'd stop by and see how you're doing. That's all."

"I'm doing all right, Carl. I— Say, I've got some coffee on inside. You want to go in and have a cup?"

"That sounds good."

Morton led the way, and the two of them went inside and sat at the table after Morton had poured two cups of coffee. Each man took a sip before anything more was said. Then Morton spoke up. "It was nice of you to stop by, Carl," he said. "I get real bored around here. I get up and try to do things, but there ain't much I can do yet. I run out of chores I can handle real quick. This is the first day that Merilee has left me alone. She's been hanging around to keep me out of trouble. She won't led me saddle a horse and ride yet."

"She's probably right, Morton. I think you ought to listen to her."

"Well, I have been. The time or two I acted like I was going to do something after she told me not to, Slocum took her part and stopped me."

"You all getting along all right with Slocum?"

"Well, sure. Why not?"

"Oh, I don't know. I just feel kind of responsible for him being here. I brought him out to my place, you know, and right off Sam Halter didn't like him. They got into a fight, so with you hurt and Merilee trying to run things, I sort of sent him over here. I don't know whose fault the fight was. I hope I done right putting him off on you and Merilee."

"Why, shucks, Carl, we ain't had no trouble with Slocum. I like Slocum, and Merilee, well, she likes him, too."

"Merilee likes him?"

"Sure. Any reason she oughtn't to?"

"No. Of course not. I was just wondering how them two was getting along. That's all."

"Oh, well, she likes him fine. Say, have you seen Slocum shoot? Man, is he good. Let me tell you . . ."

Sheriff Hardy took a ride out to the Hemp ranch. Emilie let him in and offered him coffee. He thanked her kindly and accepted it. She led him into a large room where he found Elihu sitting behind a big desk. Micah was sitting in a chair across the room from Elihu, both his arms heavily bandaged and hanging in slings. In a chair next to him, Ezra sat, carefully, on one cheek of his ass. Hardy looked at them both. He didn't bother speaking. He walked over close to Elihu's desk and pulled up a chair.

"What brings you out, Sheriff?" said Elihu.

"I'd like to say it's your pretty wife's coffee, Elihu, but I can't say that."

"What then?"

"This fight that's going on between you Hemps and Slocum. I got onto Slocum about it, but every time he's shot one of you, he's had witnesses that swear your man drew first. He said I ought to have a talk with you, and I told him I'd do that."

"So talk," Elihu said.

"I want this business to stop," said the sheriff. "I don't want to see one of your brothers or cousins shot up every day of the week. He's killed two and shot up Micah there. Ain't that enough?"

"He shot me in the ass," said Ezra.

Hardy turned sharply to look at Ezra, and Elihu gave Ezra a hard look.

"When did that happen?" said Hardy.

"Shut your mouth, Ezra, you damned fool," snapped Elihu.

Hardy looked back at Elihu. "When did Slocum shoot Ezra?" he said.

"Ezra don't know what he's talking about," Elihu said. "He took a shot out riding herd one day. Never saw who done it. He's assuming that it was Slocum. That's all."

"Elihu, I can't put up with much more of this. Now I—"

"It's all over with, Hardy," Elihu said, interrupting. "I've told all the boys to lay off of Slocum. I agree with you. I don't want any more of my kinfolks shot. He's already beat the best we had. We got no one left who could take him in a fair fight, and I don't mean to see any murder done. Slocum won't be bothered anymore by any Hemps. Does that satisfy you?"

"It does if you mean it," said Hardy.

"Of course I do. I just makes good sense."

When Hardy left the Hemp spread, he rode on over to the Hornbuckles' place. He found Morton, Merilee and Slocum all there. Merilee frowned as she invited him in. "I won't impose myself on you for long," Hardy said. "I just come from the Hemps, and old Elihu assured me that there won't be no more Hemps starting fights with Slocum there. He said it's over. I thought you all might like to know that."

"Be nice if he meant it," Merilee said.

"I believe he does," said Hardy. "He's got two killed and two shot up. You might not know it, but Ezra's shot, too. He said that you done it, Slocum, but Elihu said that they don't really know who it was done the shooting. Said Ezra was just riding herd and someone shot him from ambush."

"He's lying, Sheriff," said Slocum. "I shot a raider. I shot him right outside the house here when they come to run off the horses."

"Where'd you hit him?" asked Hardy.

"In the cheek of his ass," Slocum said.

"You've been saying there was nothing you could do about the raids on us on account of we couldn't actually identify anyone," Merilee said. "Well, by God, now we can. Ezra took a bullet in his ass, and he told you that Slocum did it. There's three of us right here that saw Slocum shoot a raider in the ass. You need more than that?"

"Well, no, I don't believe I do," Hardy said. "I'll stop by there again on my way back to town and put Ezra Hemp under arrest. There'll be a hearing scheduled."

Hardy left the house, mounted his horse and rode off. Merilee walked to the door and watched him go. Then she turned back toward Slocum and Morton. "I won't believe a damn thing he said till I see that Ezra Hemp sitting in jail."

Hardy stopped back by the Hemp ranch. Once again, Emilie opened the door. She was much surprised to see the sheriff again so soon.

"Sorry to bother you again, ma'am," he said, "but I have to see Elihu and Ezra again."

She led him back to the other room, where he found the three Hemps sitting as before.

"What is it this time, Hardy?" said Elihu, his voice betraying exasperation.

"I just stopped in on the Hornbuckles and Slocum," Hardy said. "They told me that the last time they was raided, Slocum shot a raider in the ass. There's three of them, Elihu. Three witnesses. And Ezra himself said that it was Slocum who shot him. Elihu, I'm afraid that I'm going to have to place Ezra under arrest."

"You ain't going to let him do that, are you, Elihu?" said Ezra. He sat up in his anxiousness and put weight on the wrong cheek. He howled and sat back again sideways.

"There's nothing I can do, Ezra," Elihu said. "Hardy, you don't have to take him to jail, do you? Considering the shape he's in, can't you just leave him here in my custody? There'll be a hearing, I assume. I can promise you, he'll be there."

"Well, it's kind of irregular," Hardy said, "but since it's you, I suppose it'll be all right. I'll let you know when the hearing's scheduled."

"I appreciate it," said Elihu. Hardy left again.

"What'll they do to me?" Ezra asked.

"There'll be a hearing," said Elihu. "They can't do a thing till you're found guilty. Hiram will handle everything. Even if you're found guilty, I'm not sure what the charge will be. They can't charge you with stealing horses since you never got any. Just being rowdy in the middle of the night at someone else's home. We'll likely have to pay a fine. Don't let it worry you, Ezra."

11

It was the morning of Slocum's sixth day. When his breakfast was done, he got a list of needs from Merilee and pre-
pared for a ride into town. Merilee was busy with several
household chores and did not want to go along. Morton
was anxious, though, to get out of the house, but Slocum
put him off, saying, "We can't leave Merilee here alone."
Morton grudgingly agreed. In a few more minutes, Slocum
was riding toward Hard Luck. In the meantime, Sam Halter
rode up to his earlier hiding place near the Hornbuckle
house. He cranked a shell into the chamber of his Henry rifle and settled himself in for a wait. He hoped that it would
not be a long one. In a few minutes, he saw Morton come
out of the house and fool around in the yard some. Then
Merilee stepped out the door and tossed a pan of water. He
waited a little longer. There was no sign of Slocum. Then
he studied the corral and saw no sign of the Appaloosa.
"Damn it," he said out loud. Slocum was gone somewhere.
He went back to his waiting horse and shoved the Henry
into the boot. Then he mounted up and rode toward the
herd.

Slocum made it into town and made his rounds, picking
up the goods that Merilee had ordered. He stopped by the

sheriff's office and found Hardy sitting behind his desk. The sheriff looked up from his paperwork when Slocum stepped into the office. "Howdy, Slocum," he said. "You ain't got another shooting to report, do you?"

"Just thought I'd stop by and see if maybe my money showed up yet."

"No. It ain't."

"Well, just thought I'd check."

"Slocum," said Hardy, stopping him from turning to leave. "I've got a hearing scheduled for Ezra Hemp. Just thought you might be interested. You can tell the Hornbuckles."

"I don't think that anyone'll be too interested," Slocum said. "Not till it's over and done. We'll be interested to see if anything happens to ole Ezra. I see you ain't got him in jail."

"He's been arrested," said Hardy, "but considering that he's wounded, he's in Elihu's custody. Elihu assured me that he'd show up for the hearing."

"Hardy," said Slocum, "I'd bet money that Ezra don't see one day in jail." He turned and left the sheriff's office, walking toward where he had left his horse. Up ahead on the sidewalk, Jackson hacked and coughed as he ran into the eating place. In another minute he came back out followed by Gordy Glad. Still hacking, he pointed toward Slocum. Glad gestured toward the wall behind them, and Jackson moved to lean against it and wait and watch. Glad walked out into Slocum's path. Slocum recognized the type, but he kept moving toward his horse. As he started to make a turn, Glad moved to block his path. Slocum stopped.

"You're Slocum," said Glad.

"I know that," said Slocum.

"I'm Gordy Glad."

"I don't give a shit," said Slocum.

"You ought to," said Glad. "You must have heard about me."

"I've heard."

"I heard you was in Hard Luck. I've come to kill you."

"Decided to catch me with my arms full, did you?"

"I'll let you put your bundle down," Glad said.

"That's big of you." Slocum walked on to his Appaloosa and hooked the package on the saddle horn. He walked away from the horse, keeping him out of the line of fire. "Are you working for the Hemps?" he asked.

"Never heard of them."

"Then what's your quarrel?"

"I got nothing against you, Slocum. There just ain't room for two fast guns around here. That's all."

Slocum crossed his arms over his chest. "You don't need to add to your reputation, Glad," he said. "Ride on back to the hole you crawled out of and forget it."

"Huh-uh," said Glad. "I've called you. I can't stop now. Go for your gun."

Over against the wall, Jackson started hacking again. And back behind Slocum, Hardy stepped out of his office onto the sidewalk. He stopped and watched Slocum and Glad. Glad took note of the sheriff's presence.

"Go on," he said.

"You called this show," said Slocum. "You make the first move."

"You're a cowardly shit, Slocum."

"I ain't afraid of you, Glad, but I ain't making the first move. If you want a fight, go for it. Otherwise, shut up and let me be."

"You low-crawling shitass."

Slocum turned away and walked to his horse. Without a glance back at Glad, he mounted up, turned the horse and started to ride out of town. Glad was turning red in the face from anger and frustration. He shouted after Slocum.

"Come back here and fight," he shrieked. "God damn you to hell. There'll be another time. You just wait."

Hardy started walking toward Glad, but Glad turned and hurried back into the eating house. Jackson hacked and followed him in.

Sam Halter finally figured out that the only place Slocum could have gone was to town. He rode part of the way in, to a spot on the road where he could conceal himself and have a good view of the traffic. He took his horse back into the trees a ways and tied it there. Then he moved back close to the road. The ground there rose up from the road. Halter sat down behind a big tree. He found himself looking down on the road. Everything was quiet. He held his Henry rifle where he could bring it into play easily and quickly. After sitting and waiting for a few minutes, he got bored and rolled a smoke and lit it. Still he watched the road. His back still hurt where the barbed wire had cut him. It was a constant reminder of his purpose. He was bored, but he was determined. He would wait there all day if he had to.

His mind wandered to the luscious Merilee Hornbuckle. He longed to slip up on her and show her what a real man could do. He tried to picture her naked. He imagined her laid out on her bed, her legs spread and himself snuggling down between them, probing her wet cunt. God damn Carl Doaks. If he was too chicken shit to let her know his feelings, why then, why should he not enjoy her body himself. But not Slocum. Not that son of a bitch. He was determined to kill Slocum and then to have his way with Merilee. No one would dream that the deed had been done by Halter. Everyone knew that the Hemps were after Slocum. They would get the blame. It would be perfect. He had no use for the Hemps anyway. His bullet would do double duty. He watched the road carefully. There was a curve just ahead that Slocum would come riding around. As soon as he appeared, that would be the time to shoot. He lit another smoke and waited.

Slocum came riding up to the curve in the road, and just as he making the turn, he noticed a wisp of smoke rising up from off to one side. Not stopping, he dismounted, slapped the Appaloosa on the rump and said, "Keep going, big fella." As the horse moved on, he slipped his Winchester out of the boot and cranked a shell into the chamber.

Halter heard the sound of approaching hoofbeats. He tossed aside his smoke and raised the rifle to his shoulder. His heartbeat increased as he waited. When the riderless Appaloosa appeared, his eyes opened wide. He panicked. Where the hell was Slocum? Had someone beat him to the punch? One of the Hemps? Had they knocked Slocum out of the saddle?

Slocum moved into cover on the opposite side of the road from where he had seen the smoke. He moved cautiously forward. He did not know who might be hidden up there. It could be one of the Hemps, or it could be that snake Halter. He had left Glad back in town, and there was no way that Glad could have gotten ahead of him. It might not be anyone, but the smoke was suspicious. He moved ahead a little farther. Stopping and studying the far side of the road, he once more saw the small wisp of smoke rising. He had the spot pinpointed. Looking around, he found a stick. He picked it up, took off his hat and placed the hat on the end of the stick. Then crawling on his belly and keeping the stick low, he moved ahead a little more. Reaching out the length of his arm, he uprighted the stick, pushing the hat up above the brush. Then he backed off again, leaving the stick propped up.

Halter spotted the hat. He raised his rifle and took careful aim. His palms were sweating, and his heart was pounding. He aimed below the hat and squeezed the trigger. The rifle report resounded throughout space. The hat did not move. He fired again, and the hat disappeared. Had he hit his mark? He waited. No shot answered his two. He must have killed Slocum. If Slocum were still alive, he would be returning fire. Slowly, cautiously, he stood up. He strained to get a better look, but he could see nothing. He chambered another round and began moving slowly down the slope toward the road. He reached the edge of his cover and stopped. His eyes searched the side of the road across the way. He could see no movement. After about a minute, he moved out into the open.

Slocum stood up across the road, rifle ready. Halter stopped, and his heart almost stopped as well. "So it's you, Sam," Slocum said. "Throw down that rifle." Halter stood still, trying to decide what to do. "Drop it," said Slocum. Halter started to do as he'd been told, but at the last second he made a dangerous decision. Quickly, he raised the Henry to his shoulder, but before he could pull the trigger, Slocum fired his Winchester. The slug tore into Halter's chest. He staggered back a few steps, stumbling and falling to one side, dropping the rifle as he fell. Slocum walked across to look down on Halter. He was not dead, but he was in bad shape. He looked up at Slocum with wide eyes. His mouth was hanging open. There was a bloody hole in the middle of his chest. His breath was raspy. Slocum shook his head.

"What the hell were you trying to prove, Sam?" he said. He bent down to take the six-gun out of Halter's holster and toss it aside. Then he kicked the rifle away. The man was still alive, and he might find the strength to try another shot. Slocum turned to walk away.

"Slocum," said Halter in a weak voice. "You just going to leave me like this?"

Slocum paused and looked back over his shoulder. "What were your plans for me, Sam?" he said. He walked on down to the road and started after his horse. Sam Halter would not live much longer.

•   •   •

Slocum stopped by the Hornbuckle place long enough to deliver the package of goods Merilee had ordered. He told the Hornbuckles that he had an errand to run over to Doaks's place, and that he would return shortly. Then he rode on, leaving brother and sister looking after him with curiosity. In a few minutes, he rode up to Doaks's house. Doaks came out to meet him.

"Slocum," he said, "what's up?"

"Sam Halter just tried to ambush me," Slocum said. "I left him laying beside the road back yonder a few miles. Just wanted to let you know."

"Is he dead?"

"He wasn't. He might be by now."

Doaks hurried toward his corral. As he was saddling his horse, he said to Slocum," I don't suppose you think I had anything to do with this?"

"It never crossed my mind, Carl," said Slocum.

Doaks cinched up his saddle and mounted. He started riding toward the road. "You coming with me?" he said.

"Nope," said Slocum. "I'm finished with him."

Doaks rode on ahead, and Slocum took his time going back to the Hornbuckle ranch.

"What you going to do next?" said Jackson, between coughs.

Across the table in the saloon, Glad did not answer. He picked up his glass and took a drink of whiskey.

"If Slocum won't fight you, what are you going to do?"

"He'll fight," said Glad. "Sooner or later, he'll fight. He was just pulling the same stunt that I was pulling on him. He wanted to make me draw first. Well, I ain't going to fall for that. Not in town with the sheriff standing behind him. I ain't that dumb."

Jackson had a sudden hacking fit, and once again, Glad was afraid that the man would not survive it. At last it passed. Tears were streaming down Jackson's face, and he wiped them away with his coat sleeve. Then he picked up his glass and took a long swallow of whiskey.

"If he won't draw first, and you won't draw first, then how are you going to have a shoot-out with him?" he asked.

"I'll figure something out," said Glad. "Don't you worry about it."

"Hey," said Jackson, looking and pointing toward the big window on the front wall of the saloon. "Carl Doaks is hauling in a corpse."

Glad turned to look and caught a glimpse of a body slung across a saddle just before it moved on past the window. He tossed down his drink and got up. Jackson stood up cluthing his bottle. He downed the rest of the whiskey in his glass and followed Glad out the door. They stood on the sidewalk and watched Doaks stop at the sheriff's office. "Go see who it is," said Glad. Hacking, Jackson hurried toward the sheriff's office.

Hardy had seen Doaks ride up. He did not wait for Doaks to come inside, but went out to meet him. He saw the body slung across the second horse. "Who is it, Carl?" he asked.

"It's Sam Halter," said Doaks.

Jackson went into a spasm of coughing, and Hardy looked at him with disgust. "Get on out of here, Jackson," he said. "This ain't none of your business."

Jackson hacked and staggered and finally sucked in a deep breath.

"He tried to bushwhack Slocum," Doaks said, "but Slocum got the better of it."

"Slocum again," said Hardy. "The death rate sure went up around here when that son of a bitch rode into town. Did you see it happen?"

"No, but—"

"Then how the hell do you know it happened like that?"

"When I come across Sam," said Doaks, "he was still alive. Just barely. He admitted to me how it happened."

"How'd you happen across him?"

"Slocum came by the house and told me," said Doaks.

Jackson hacked and turned to walk away. He headed back toward where Glad waited just outside the Hard Luck Saloon.

"Slocum left him laying there to bleed to death and went and told you?" said Hardy.

"I'm afraid he did," said Doaks. "I rode on out there and found Sam still alive. He told me before he died what happened."

"And he said that he ambushed Slocum?"

"Yes. He did."

Hardy shook his head slowly. "I don't know how one man can kill so many men and still keep it all legal."

Across the street, Jackson told Glad, "It's a fella named Sam Halter. He used to work for Carl Doaks. That's Carl what brung him in. He tried to kill Slocum, but Slocum got him first."

"So Slocum killed the poor bastard?" said Glad.

"Yeah," said Jackson. "That's right."

"Where is Slocum?"

"I don't know," said Jackson. He was suddenly hit by another fit. When it subsided, he said, "He's likely out at the Hornbuckle place."

12

Slocum was out riding the Hornbuckle range near the boundary line between Hornbuckle and Hemp. He found some Hemp cattle and rounded them up, then started riding the fence line. He came across the place where the fence was down, ran the cattle back through to the proper side and then set about mending the fence. It was late afternoon, and he did not want to lounge around the house with Merilee and Morton. He figured there was work to be done, and finding the Hemp cattle on the Hornbuckle range had proved him correct. The Hornbuckle cattle were all still mixed in with Doaks's bunch and were grazing at the other end of the property. He was glad that he had ridden out to check on things. He had the posts all secured and was stringing the top wire, the last of the loose wires, when he saw the riders coming at him. Quickly, he tacked the wire in place and moved back to his waiting Appaloosa and the Winchester rifle. There was no sense in taking any chances.

Ferdie Hemp was leading a bunch of the Hemp hands out on a routine check of the cattle when they came across the small bunch that Slocum had driven back across to their own range. They stopped riding and studied the cattle for a moment, then looked toward the fence and spotted Slocum.

"Reckon what these cows are doing way over here?" said one of the riders.

"Ain't no telling," said Ferdie. "I'm more interested in what Slocum's doing over yonder."

"Looked to me like he was mending the fence," said the rider. "Likely our cows got over there, and he driv them back. Then he went and restrung the wires."

"Could be," said Ferdie. "But look, we got him way outnumbered."

"Elihu said we was to leave him alone."

Ferdie thought about Elihu and about Gordy Glad, but he considered that if he and his crew should get Slocum first, he would save Elihu five hundred dollars. He couldn't imagine that Elihu would be upset by that, or by the fact that they actually got Slocum. And after all, they had not gone out looking for Slocum. They had just happened on him. It was good fortune, that's what it was.

"Look, boys," he said, "if we was to take after him right now direct, he could head back for the house, where he might have some help and some witnesses. We don't want neither of them."

"So what do we do?"

"Let's just ignore him," said Ferdie. "Let's ride casual-like back in that direction. Drive these here cows as we go. That way, when we cross the fence, we'll cut him off from his path back to the house."

Slocum watched as the riders moved away from him. They were riding slowly. Maybe they did not want any trouble that day. Maybe. He mounted his horse and sat and watched them for a bit. They seemed to be ignoring him. They were driving the cattle somewhere. Maybe this bunch had gotten separated from the main herd, and they were taking them back where they belonged. At last he was satisfied that the Hemp riders were not interested in him that day. He decided that he would finish the job he had started. He turned back to the fence and continued his ride. He wanted to be sure that the entire fence line between the two properties was secure. In another couple of minutes, he could no longer see the riders.

Ferdie called a halt. Slocum was out of sight. He had ridden away from the ranch house, and that was good. Ferdie congratulated himself on his ploy of using the cattle. He had surely fooled Slocum with that one. "All right," he said, "it's time to cross the fence. Let's tear it down right here." He took his lariat and swung a loop, hooking one of the fence posts. Two of his riders did the same. With their ropes dallied around the saddle horns, they pulled until the posts came up out of the ground. They dragged them away a distance. Then they rode through to the Hornbuckle side. "Now," said Ferdie, "if he sees us coming at him, we'll be between him and the house. All he can do is run or turn and fight. As soon as he's in range, start shooting." He led off at a gallop, thinking as he rode of how Elihu would congratulate him once the deed had been done.

Slocum was not finding any more trouble spots in the fence. He kept riding, wondering how far the line would continue. He had not been on this part of the range before. Up ahead he could see rugged hills rising out of the prairie. They were rocky and spotted with clumps of scrubby trees and brush. Then he came across the creek, the water supply that Hemp was apparently so jealous of on the Hornbuckle spread. He figured that he must be wandering close to the source of the supply. The water must be coming from somewhere up in the hills. Behind the first line of hills, he could see another rising up. This was interesting country. He would enjoy checking it out. Suddenly his big Appaloosa nickered and shook his head.

"What is it?" Slocum said.

The horse tossed his head and seemed to be trying to look back behind. Slocum stopped riding and let the big stallion have his head. The Appaloosa turned around and stretched his neck and whinnied loud. Then Slocum spotted the approaching riders. It was the same bunch he had seen earlier, and they were riding hard at him.

"Damn," he said. "I let them sucker me."

He turned his horse again and headed for the hills in front of him. There were too many to stand and fight face to face.

Back on his trail, Ferdie cursed. "He's seen us," he said. One of the riders fired a rifle shot at Slocum. "Save your bullets," Ferdie said. "He's too far ahead. Come on. Let's get him." The Hemp bunch started riding hard.

Slocum let the Appaloosa stretch his legs, and the big animal was also stretching out the distance between him and the pursuing riders. "That's it, fella," said Slocum. "Leave them behind."

"He's gaining on us," one of the Hemp riders shouted.

"Well, he can't run forever," answered Ferdie. "Keep a-going."

Slocum at last reached the first range of hills. He stopped, looked back at the riders, then studied the hill ahead. He spotted what looked to be a good path going up toward the top. It was a clear space winding its way between the jutting boulders and clumps of thick brush. He urged the Appaloosa forward, and it started taking the hill with no problems. About halfway up, he passed a thicket and thought about stopping and hiding back behind it and waiting for the bastards, but he decided against it and kept going. Finally he reached the top. He turned to look back behind him and saw that the riders were almost to the bottom of the hill. He was a sitting duck where he had stopped, and, in fact, two of the riders pulled rifles and leveled them at him. He turned and headed for the far side as two shots rang out.

"Let's get up there," said Ferdie. He rode the same path that Slocum had taken, and several of his riders followed him. Others sought out other ways to the top. They swarmed up the hill with blood in their craws. "Watch out," Ferdie shouted. "He might be laying in ambush somewhere up there." He reached the top of the hill safely, though, and, wisely, he waited for the rest to arrive. When they were back together in a bunch, he said, "It looks to me like he's gone down the other side. He'll be down there in that valley or else heading up the next hill."

"I see him," shouted one of the riders, pointing. Sure enough, Slocum was down between the two ranges of hills, riding away from them toward their right.

"Let's see if we can pick him off from here," Ferdie said, dismounting and pulling out his rifle. The others followed his example. Some of them knelt, one or two lay down close to the edge of the top of the hill, and some stood upright, but soon they were all firing.

Bullets whizzed by close to Slocum, kicked up dust near his horse's feet and seemed to fill the air like a swarm of insects. He kicked the Appaloosa in the sides, and the big horse leaped forward. It moved fast down the valley and around a clump of big rocks. The firing stopped.

Up on top of the hill, Ferdie stood looking after Slocum, even though Slocum was now out of his sight. "Damn it," he said. "Why couldn't no one hit him?"

"It was a long shot, Ferdie."

"Yeah. Yeah." He stomped back to his horse and shoved the rifle in the boot. "Mount up," he said. "Let's get after him."

He started down the side of the hill too quickly, and his horse stumbled, tossing him off over its head. He screamed as he flew through the air and landed hard, scraping his face and one side of his body on the rocky ground. He rolled to one side just in the nick of time as his horse came rolling after him and screaming like a stuck pig. Neighing frantically, the horse managed to get back to its feet and hurry on down to the bottom of the hill. Ferdie struggled to his own feet. He checked to make sure no bones were broken. "Son of a bitch," he snarled.

"Are you all right?" someone called.

"Hell, I'll live." Ferdie started walking down the hill after his horse. He slipped and slid, but at last he made it. The horse trotted off when he approached it. The other riders, having seen Ferdie's mishap, moved down the hill much more slowly. When they finally made it to the bottom, one of them rode after and caught up with Ferdie's nervous mount and brought it back to him. Cursing, he mounted up again. Again, he had his riders all gathered together. After his unfortunate tumble, he was more determined than ever to catch and kill Slocum.

"All right," he said. "He's right up that way. Let's go."

They started riding in pursuit of Slocum, but this time they moved more slowly, watching the trail ahead and the hills on both sides of them. Ferdie pulled out his rifle again and held it ready as he rode.

Slocum knew that the riders were not far behind, and he knew that he did not want to fight them. He was far too outnumbered. The only way he would fight was if they cornered him, and he intended to do everything he could to avoid that. He was thinking about riding up and over the next hill, but he saw an easy way back up the same hill he had already crossed. The Hemp bunch was down in the valley behind him. If he recrossed the hill, he would have his way to the ranch house clear. He would turn the tables on them. He took the way up the side of the hill to his right, headed back toward the ranch house.

Ferdie rounded a light curve and halted his gang. He looked carefully at the hills on both sides. There were big boulders and clumps of scrubby trees and patches of thick brush. Slocum could be hiding behind any of it, waiting in ambush. If he were to start shooting, he could get several of them before the rest got him, and Ferdie was keenly aware that he would most likely be one of the first to fall. It was an uncomfortable feeling. Keeping his voice low, but strong enough to be heard by most of his riders, he said, "Anyone see anything up there?"

He waited a spell but he got no response. A deer jumped out from behind a thicket of brush on the hillside to the left, and four rifle shots sounded. No one hit it. It made it to the next hiding spot safely.

"Damn it," said Ferdie. "That was just a damn deer. Don't be so jumpy."

He knew that Slocum had heard the shots, and since they had not come near him, he would also know that his pursuers were getting nervous. Ferdie did not like that.

"All right," he said. "Stay ready, but don't shoot unless you see Slocum. Come on now. Let's move on ahead."

Slocum was some distance ahead of the Hemp riders and about halfway up the hillside. He almost rode on, but he stopped to study a large rock that seemed to be just sitting there loose on the hillside. He moved ahead, up above the rock, and stopped again, dismounting. He let the reins of his Appaloosa trail on the ground and studied the lay of the land below. There were other rocks down there, rocks that were in the path of the loose one he had stopped to study. He moved behind the big rock and tested it with a slight shove. He was pretty sure that he could dislodge it. He decided to sit there and wait. He took out a cigar and a match and lit his smoke. Let them spot him. He didn't care anymore.

Sure enough, Ferdie spotted the plume of smoke rising from Slocum's cigar. He halted his column and studied the smoke with curiosity. What kind of gall was that, he wondered. It sure enough looked like someone was sitting there smoking. Slocum had been running from them. Did he have such a good spot picked out that he actually thought he could fight them all off? Ferdie had not thought Slocum

to be so much of a fool. But it couldn't be anyone but
Slocum.

"Get off your horses," he said. All the riders dismounted, taking their rifles with them. "Come on," Ferdie
said. Ducking low, he began walking ahead. He paused
along the way and pointed toward the plume of smoke.
"See that?" he said. There were murmurs of affirmation behind him. "That's got to be him just setting there waiting
for us. We're going to move on up till we're right under
him, but keep low. He'll likely be expecting us to be riding.
We might can get there without being seen. Once we're in
place, we'll start shooting."

Staying low, Ferdie led the way. He moved with cau-
tion, stopping every now and then to look back up the hill
for the telltale smoke. At last he found himself right below
the big rock, and he signaled the rest to stop and stay low.
He looked up the side of the hill, but he could see nothing
but the smoke. At least the son of a bitch was still there. He
spoke to his followers in a hoarse whisper.

"See that big rock up there? He's right around it somewheres. Cut loose."

They all started shooting at once.

Slocum was behind the big rock. He sat still, smoking,
and let them shoot for a while. At last he put his feet
against the rock and shoved with all his might. It rocked.
He shoved again. He could hear the ground and the gravel
beneath the rock crunch and scrape. He shoved again, and
the rock rolled. It tumbled and stopped.

"Hey," someone shouted down below. "Watch out."

Slocum scurried down to the big rock and shoved again.
It started to roll again. This time it tore through some
brush. It picked up speed. It jarred other rocks loose in its
path. It kicked up a dust screen behind it in its wake, and
Slocum hurried on over to where his big Appaloosa waited
patiently. The path ahead was steep, so he took the reins
and walked ahead of the horse, leading it up toward the

top. Below him the big rock was still rolling, and it was picking up more and more rocks as it went.

Some of the Hemp riders turned to run back in the direction they had come from, but they ran into their horses and then into each other. Others ran the other direction, running over Ferdie. One of two just looked up in unbelieving astonishment at the avalanche bearing down on them.

"God damn," someone shouted.

"Let me out of here."

Some small rocks reached the bottom before the big one, and they bounced off of the heads and backs and shoulders of some of the Hemp crew. The horses began to panic and try to figure a way out of the trap they were in. Some few ran partway up the sides of the hills. The big rock at last came to a stop down in the valley. The landslide was over. Horses were still milling and neighing. Men were groaning and cursing. Slowly the dust settled, and the men began standing up and dusting themselves off and checking for any serious injuries. Most had bruises and some small cuts, but at last they discovered that the big rock had come to rest on top of Ferdie's right leg.

"Get it offa me," Ferdie moaned. "Get it off. It's killing me."

Four men put their shoulders to the big rock and pushed and shoved as Ferdie screamed with pain. At last they rolled it off. Ferdie's leg was a mess. It was going to be a long and slow ride home.

13

It was late when Slocum made it back to the Hornbuckle place, but Merilee and Morton were both still up. It was obvious to both Hornbuckles that Slocum was well nigh done in. He dropped heavily into a chair at the table, and Merilee quickly went for the bottle that they had stashed on a shelf. She poured Slocum a drink of whiskey and placed the bottle on the table. He gulped down his drink and poured another. Then he let out a heavy sigh of relief.

"All right," said Merilee, "what happened?"

Slocum told the tale of the Hemp bunch chasing him and what he finally did to them.

"Was any of them killed?" said Morton, anxious.

"I didn't wait around to find out," said Slocum. "I dropped the rocks on them and took off like a scared jackrabbit."

"We're coming fast to an open range war," Merilee said.

"Let it come," said Morton. "I'm ready for it." Slocum took another sip of whiskey, and Morton said, "The dirty bastards."

"Watch your goddamn language," said Merilee.

"Oh, all right," Morton said. "But they are."

"That's beside the point," said Merilee. "Mama and Daddy raised you better than that."

"You mean I can kill them, but I can't cuss them?"

"That's about the size of it."

"Well, I doubt if they'll be around anytime soon," said Slocum. "I'd bet that most of them that was after me are banged up some."

"We'll be ready for them when they do show up," said Merilee.

"What are we waiting for?" said Morton. "Why don't we go ahead and hit them while they're crippled up?"

"That's not a bad idea," Slocum agreed. "It would sure be the time for it, all right."

"I don't want to be the one to start a range war," said Merilee.

"I'd say they done started it by going after Slocum the way they done," said Morton.

"Well," Merilee said, "you might be right, but let's sleep on it and talk about it again in the morning."

Two of the Hemp horses were crippled by the landslide and had to be shot. One rider had a broken arm. Another had had his fingers smashed. Ferdie's leg was so badly smashed there was no way he could sit a horse. Some of the more fortunate riders, that is the ones with only cuts and bruises, tried to set the broken bone and rig up a splint, but they did a poor job of it. They tied it up anyway. Then they did the same with the other man's broken arm, but they did a little better job of that. They had no idea what to do about the smashed fingers. Finally they had to decide how they were going to get back to the ranch house. Someone suggested they rig up a travois for Ferdie, but they couldn't locate any suitable branches. Finally they slung him across a saddle and tied his hands to his good leg underneath the horse to keep him on. He was screaming the whole time.

"You're killing me," he shouted. "You're doing me worse than what Slocum did. My goddamn leg's going to fall off."

There was no way around it, they said. He would have to suffer the pain or lay out there in the valley alone while they went for help, and they couldn't figure out what anyone else could do out there any better than what they had done. With the two dead horses and Ferdie tied across a third, there were two men without mounts. They had to double up. At last they were ready to ride, but the first thing they had to do was get up the hillside. They had to ride some of the horses partway up and around the fallen boulders to get everyone back together. Then they had to ride the valley for a ways to find a way up. At last they got started. The two horses carrying double could barely make it, so the extra riders had to get off and walk up the hillside. The man with the broken arm had a hard time keeping his saddle, so he, too, got off and walked. There was considerable slipping and sliding, but the most miserable of all was poor wretched Ferdie.

"I ain't going to live to see the top of this hill," he shouted. "You're killing me. I'm getting sick. I'm going to puke."

They reached the top at last, and they had to stop and take a rest. Ferdie made them untie him and let him down, but he screamed with pain when they dragged him off the saddle and stretched him out on the ground. They drank some water from their canteens, and some of the men rolled smokes and lit them. Ferdie begged someone to roll him one. At last they were ready to tackle going down the other side of the hill. "Boys," said Ferdie, "I can't stand it the way you had me all trussed up like that. Just set me in the saddle. I can take it." Two of the men picked him up and lifted him until he could swing his good leg across his horse's back, but when he settled down in the saddle, the pain was excruciating. He howled. "Get me offa here. I can't stand it." They dragged him off again, while he shrieked some more. One of the riders, George Mackey, was getting disgusted. He took a final drag off his cigarette and tossed the butt.

"We'll be out here all goddamn night at this rate," he

said. "Come on. Let's sling him back across the saddle and tie him the way we done before."

"That hurts too goddamn bad," said Ferdie. "I can't go all the way back home like that."

"You can't sit in the fucking saddle," said Mackey. "What the hell do you want us to do with you? Shoot you like a crippled horse?"

Mackey and two other hands grabbed Ferdie and tossed him belly down across the saddle again. As they tied him down, he screamed until he was out of breath, and then he whimpered and whined. At last they started moving again. The way down was about as rough as the way up had been. One horse took a tumble, and horse and rider slid about halfway down the hillside. Both managed to regain their feet, seemingly unhurt, and get the rest of the way down safely. All except Ferdie were greatly relieved when they at last reached the bottom. The way home was at least flat from there on. It was still going to be a good long ride, though, especially for Ferdie.

It was late night when Gordy Glad and Jackson rode up close to the Hornbuckle spread. They could see the house from the road. The moon was out bright and lit up the night sky pretty well. They could even make out the Appaloosa in the corral.

"He's here all right," said Jackson. "I can see that big spotty-ass horse over there."

He hacked and spat.

"Try to keep quiet," said Glad. "They might hear you."

"We ain't too close to the house," Jackson protested.

"Sound carries at night," said Glad.

"Are you going to go down there and kill him?"

"Not now," said Glad. "If I was to bother them folks in their own house in the middle of the night, it would likely be seen as a clear case of murder. No. We're going to spend the night right here and be ready for him in the morning."

"We're going to sleep out here?" said Jackson.

"That's right," said Glad. "Don't worry. You'll be just fine." He reached into his saddlebag and pulled out a bottle which he handed to Jackson. Jackson took it greedily and uncorked it. He sucked a long drink from the bottle before he lowered it from his lips. Glad moved to the side of the road opposite the Hornbuckle house and then led the horses back into the brush and tied them there. Then he moved on foot back close to the road, to a spot where he could watch the house. He spread his blanket on the ground and told Jackson to do the same. Jackson settled down to drink himself into a stupor.

Elihu Hemp was furious when his riders showed up at the house. He had been asleep, and so, of course, had been his lady. When he saw the condition of Ferdie, his rage subsided long enough to order someone to ride into town for the doctor. When the rider was gone, he turned loose his rage again, directly at Ferdie. "What the hell were you thinking?" he shouted. "Just what the hell were you thinking? I gave direct orders that no one was to attack Slocum again. To leave it all to that Glad. You were in charge of those riders, Ferdie. You're to blame. You alone. You went against my orders, and look what the hell it got for you."

"I'm dying over here, Elihu," Ferdie whimpered. "Don't be fussing at me now."

All of the riders were sitting around in the big room that served as Elihu's office. They were all in need of some patching up. Emilie poured drinks all around. She did what she could for them, daubing at small wounds. Elihu paced the floor fuming. His face was bright red with anger. He was wondering what Sheriff Hardy would do if Slocum were to lodge a complaint. He already had a hearing scheduled for Ezra. Now Ferdie had pulled this fool stunt. And there was no reason for it. Glad was in town. He would take care of Slocum. He was a professional.

"My leg's killing me," whined Ferdie.

Emilie mopped his brow with a damp cloth. She glanced at the leg, but she knew that there was nothing she could do for it. They would just have to wait for the doctor. Ezra hobbled into the room leaning on a crutch and took a long and hard look at Ferdie's leg.

"My God," he said. "That's bad. What the hell did Slocum do? Drop a mountain on you? I thought I had it bad till I seen that. God almighty, that's a ugly son of a bitch."

"Oh God," whined Ferdie.

"Shut up, Ezra," said Elihu. "You're just making things worse."

"All I said was—"

"I said shut up."

Ezra looked around the room for a place to sit. He finally spotted one and hobbled over to it, sitting down gingerly on just one cheek of his ass. He continued to stare at Ferdie. Elihu walked over to stand just behind Emilie. He put a hand on her shoulder.

"Emilie," he said, "you've done all you can do here. Go on back to bed. I'll wait up for the doctor."

She stood up and turned to face him. "I'm all right, dear," she said. "I might be able to be of some use. I'll stay."

"Well then," Elihu said, "why don't you put on a pot of coffee. It looks like it's going to be a long night."

Jackson passed out, the whiskey bottle cradled in his left arm. Glad glanced over at him and at the bottle. He wanted a drink, but he had only brought the one bottle. He thought about the nasty little man hacking and coughing, and he could not bring himself to drink from the same bottle as the wretch had been sucking on. He would probably catch something horrible and die of it, a slow and lingering death. He decided that he could wait till sometime the following day. He looked back toward the ranch house. All was still dark. It would be for a while yet. He stretched himself out on his blanket to try to get a little sleep.

Doc Grubbs finally showed up at the Hemp ranch, and he walked into the house grumbling about being dragged out of bed in the middle of the night. When he walked into Elihu's office, he stopped and looked around at the battered bunch. "My God," he said, "what got after all of them?"

"Never mind that, Doc," said Elihu. "Just get to work. Ferdie there is the worst off."

"Your rider told me that he had a bad busted leg," said Doc. He walked over to where Ferdie lay moaning.

"It's killing me, Doc," Ferdie said.

Doc bent over and looked at the leg. He made a face. "I'd say so," he said. "Who done this to you?"

"It was a rock slide," said Elihu quickly, not wanting any unnecessary information getting out too early.

"Well, it's bad, all right," said Doc. "I can't patch that up. It'll have to come off."

"Are you sure?" Elihu asked.

Ferdie half sat up, his face turned pale and his mouth agape. "You going to chop off my leg?" he said.

"You got a choice," said Doc. "You could just lay here and die."

"Oh. Oh, my God," Ferdie moaned.

Doc reached in his bag for a bottle. He brought it out and handed it to Ferdie. "Here," he said. "Drink this."

"What is it?" Ferdie asked.

"Laudanum," said Doc. "Drink it down." He got up and moved over to the man with the broken arm.

"What about Ferdie?" said Elihu.

"I got to let that stuff take effect," said Doc. "While I'm waiting, I'll deal with these others."

He unwrapped the arm, reset it and wrapped it back up again. Then he began moving around the room checking the other more minor wounds, patching up cuts and scrapes. Emilie offered him a cup of coffee, and he accepted. In a couple of minutes, she brought it to him. He took a sip, put the cup down and got back to his work. As he finished with each man, Elihu sent the man on back to the bunkhouse. Finally there was no one left except Ferdie. Doc stood up and took a long look at the sorry leg. He looked back at Elihu.

"I need him laid out on a table," he said. "And I'll need good light."

Elihu swept the papers and other things off his big desktop, and he and Doc and Emilie moved the now benumbed Ferdie over there and stretched him out on the bare desk.

"Lots of rags," said Doc. "Hot water." He looked at the bottle he had given to Ferdie and saw that it was still half-full. He lifted Ferdie's head and held the bottle to his lips. "Drink up," he said. "Come on." Ferdie mumbled some unintelligible words and drank.

"Couldn't that stuff kill him?" Elihu said.

"It might," said Doc, "but without it, the pain of what I've got to do will damn sure kill him. Elihu, you've got to stop your boys from trying to kill that Slocum."

"Who said anything about Slocum?" said Elihu. "I told you this happened in a landslide."

"I know what you told me, but I also know what's been going on out here and in town. I've patched up Ezra and Micah now. Asa and Eben are dead. Are you trying to get your whole damn family wiped out?"

"Just do your job here, Doc, and mind your own business."

"Well, I guess that's telling it to me straight enough," said Doc. He drank the rest of the coffee out of his cup and set the cup down. Emilie brought in a pan of hot water and set it down on a small table near the desk. She had a bundle of rags over her shoulder. She put those on the table as well. Doc looked at Ferdie, who appeared to be in a drunken stupor. "Well," he said, "no use putting it off any longer." He reached into his bag and pulled out a short saw. He looked up at Emilie. "Ma'am," he said, "you might want to leave the room."

14

Slocum saddled up his Appaloosa on the seventh day of his wait and headed into Hard Luck. As he rode through the main gate to the Hornbuckle place and out onto the road, he saw Gordy Glad step out into his path. He halted his mount. Glad threw back his coattails to reveal two ivory-handled Colts ready for action. Slocum sagged in his saddle as if he were tired and glared at the man.

"Gordy," he said, "I've got enough trouble around here with the Hemps. I don't need no more from you."

"I'm here to kill you, Slocum," said Glad. "I'll let you get down off your horse and get set. I won't take advantage of you."

"Well, I ain't going to do it," said Slocum.

"Why not?"

"Because I don't want to. That's why."

"But I brought me a witness out here and everything. I'm all ready to go. You can't do me this way, Slocum."

"I don't see why not. I've got business in town, Gordy. You're holding me up."

"I mean to do worse than that. I mean to kill you. Damn it."

"Do you mean to murder me?"

"I don't do murders. You know that. Now get down off that horse and fight me." Slocum urged the Appaloosa forward and rode around Glad, tipping his hat as he did. "Like I said, I got business in town. I expect I'll be seeing you around though."

Glad stood in the middle of the road with his jaw sagging and his eyes wide in disbelief. This had never happened to him before. Even when other men had thought of it and tried to do it, they had finally panicked and gone for their guns. Slocum had a cool head all right. Finally Glad yelled, "Jackson. Get your ass out here." His immediate answer was a fit of coughing, but finally Jackson emerged from the brush and came staggering out in the road.

"What is it?" he said, and he coughed again.

"Go on back there and bring out our horses."

Jackson staggered back into the brush and disappeared, but Glad could still hear him hacking. He wished he had found a different witness, someone not quite so disgusting as this puke. But he was cheap. In another minute, Jackson emerged again, this time leading two horses. Glad mounted up and started to ride. Jackson was slower. When he at last got in the saddle, he hurried to catch up to Glad. Riding alongside him, he said, "Where we going? Back to town? We're out of whiskey, you know."

"Lead me to Elihu Hemp's house," said Glad.

Emilie Hemp answered the door, and Gordy Glad took off his hat. "Howdy, ma'am," he said. Jackson was coughing, but he finally got back some control.

"We come to see Elihu, Miz Hemp," he said.

Emilie did not want Jackson in her house, and she knew that Elihu did not want him in either. She motioned toward the chairs on the porch. "Have a seat," she said. "I'll fetch him out." She shut the door before she disappeared back into the house. Jackson took a seat, but Glad paced the porch. In another minute, Elihu Hemp came out. Jackson stood up and nodded.

"Hello, Jackson," Elihu said.

Jackson gave a little nod of the head and said, "Hello, Mr. Hemp." Then he began to cough. Hemp turned to face Glad.

"I don't believe I've had the pleasure," he said.

"I'm Glad."

"Glad of what? I don't understand."

"I'm Gordy Glad," said Glad, a bit miffed.

"Oh," said Elihu. "Oh, of course. Gordy Glad. Well, just what are you doing here? I told Ferdie that I did not want to see you, and I did not want you coming around here."

"Some things have happened," said Glad.

"What are you talking about?"

"I've faced Slocum twice now. The son of a bitch won't fight me."

"Is he scared of you?"

"Not him. He just won't fight. I've got to have a man draw on me before I kill him."

"I see," said Elihu. He sat down in one of the chairs and put his chin in his hand.

"Just what the hell am I supposed to do?" said Glad.

Suddenly Elihu straightened up. He looked directly at Glad. "I've got it," he said. "Go after the girl."

"What girl?"

"The Hornbuckle girl," said Elihu. "I've heard it said that Slocum's sweet on her. He's living with her and her brother. Threaten her, and he'll fight."

When Slocum rode into Hard Luck, Sheriff Hardy saw him coming and stepped out into the street to wave him down. Slocum stopped riding and looked down at the sheriff. "What is it this time?" he said.

"I want to talk to you," said Hardy. "Come into my office."

Slocum pulled over to the rail, dismounted and tied the

Appaloosa. Then he followed Hardy into the office. The sheriff walked immediately behind his desk and sat down. Slocum pulled up a chair and sat. "What's on your mind?" he said.

"You," said Hardy. "Always you."

"Four more days and I'll be gone," said Slocum. "If that money gets here when it should."

"It'll be here," said Hardy.

"Then your worries will be over. Anything else?"

"What the hell did you do to Ferdie Hemp and his boys? Doc come in here and told me that he'd had to cut off Ferdie's leg. The rest of the boys looked like hash."

"They were chasing me over on Hornbuckle land," said Slocum. "Trying to kill me. I just rolled some rocks down on them is all."

"That's all? I'd say it was more than enough."

"They had me powerful outnumbered, Sheriff," said Slocum. "I wouldn't have had a chance shooting it out with them."

Hardy looked at his desktop and shook his head. "Four more days," he said.

"You laid out the schedule," said Slocum. "I'm just going by what you told me."

"Get out of here."

Slocum went to the general store and bought a few cigars and a box of .45 shells. Then he went over to the Hard Luck Saloon and ordered a drink of brown whiskey with the last of his money. He could easily go for four days with no cash. He'd gone much longer than that before. He lifted the glass and sniffed it. Then he took one small sip. He would make this one last awhile. Two Hemp riders came through the door and bellied up to the bar a few feet away from where Slocum stood. He recognized them, and he watched them out of the corner of his eye. They ordered beer and drank. He didn't think that they intended to start any trouble. He finished his drink and left the saloon.

• • •

Gordy Glad and Jackson rode up to the Hornbuckle house, and Morton stepped out the front door. "Howdy, Jackson," he said. "Who's that with you?"

"Friend of mine from out of town," said Jackson.

Merilee stepped out the door and looked over Morton's shoulder with curiosity.

"What can we do for you?" she said.

Jackson suffered a fit of hacking and spat a gob out on the ground. Glad made a face. Then before anyone knew what was happening, he had pulled out two Colts and leveled them at Morton and Merilee.

"Don't do anything stupid," he said.

"Oh, yeah," said Jackson. "This here is Gordy Glad. I'm sure you've heard of him."

"What do you want with us?" Merilee asked.

"I want you to walk over there by that corral," Glad said. He noted that neither of the Hornbuckles was wearing or carrying a weapon. He figured the guns were in the house. He had best get them away from the house.

"What for?" said Morton.

"Just do it," said Glad. "Go on."

The Hornbuckles started walking toward the corral. Glad, followed by Jackson, rode slowly behind them. When they reached the corral, Glad backed the two of them up against the fence. "Tie them up," he said to Jackson.

"Me?" said Jackson. "I'm just a witness. Remember?"

"You tie them up, or I'll cut your ears off."

Jackson dismounted as quickly as he could, taking the rope off his saddle. He walked tentatively toward the two Hornbuckles.

"Him first," said Glad. "Tie them to the rail there."

It took him a little while, but Jackson got his job done between fits of coughing and hacking. With the two secured, Glad holstered his Colts. Then he turned his horse and rode back to the house. He dismounted and walked inside. He stood for a moment and studied the neat little house. Then he walked to the bed and gave it a jerk, overturning it. He picked up a chair and threw it against the wall. He jerked shelves down off the wall. Now and then he tossed something out the door, so that Merilee and Morton could tell he was tearing up the house. Then he took out a match, looked around, and struck it.

Out at the corral, Morton said, "What the hell is he doing?"

Jackson started coughing. It was a major fit. Brother and sister both thought that he would fall over and die right then and there, but he was the least of their worries. Morton looked up and saw Glad coming out of their house. He mounted his horse and rode back to the corral. Then he dismounted again. He walked slowly to where the two were tied. Just then Merilee saw smoke drifting out through the door of the house.

"What have you done?" she cried.

"He's burning the house," said Morton.

"Damn you," said Merilee.

Glad slapped her hard across the face.

"Leave her alone," Morton shouted.

Glad doubled a fist and smashed it into the side of Morton's face. He slugged him again and again, until Morton sagged into unconsciousness. Merilee was screaming at Glad the whole time. Now, with Morton taken care of, Glad moved toward her. He slapped her hard twice more, and blood trickled from the corner of her mouth. Then he drew a knife from a sheath on his belt. Merilee watched it with horror. Glad reached out with his left hand and took a handful of Merilee's hair. With the knife, he sliced it off and tossed it on the ground. He took another handful and did it again. Back behind him, the flames had grown and were raging. Smoke billowed up toward the clouds in the sky.

With Merilee's hair a tousled mess, Glad began cutting at her shirt. Soon her breasts were exposed. The shirt was hanging in tattered strips from her shoulders. He put the knife away and then reached down to unfasten her jeans. He took hold of them at the waist and gave a jerk, leaving them down around her knees. Then he doubled his fist and struck her a hard blow to the side of the face. He turned and walked back to his horse. "Let's go, Jackson," he said.

Slocum was riding back toward the Hornbuckle place when he met Glad and Jackson on the road. He stopped riding, ready for anything. Glad smiled as he rode past Slocum. He tipped his hat. "You'll fight me," he said. "You can find me in town at the Hard Luck Saloon." Slocum turned in the saddle and watched Glad ride on. He wondered what the hell the bastard was talking about. He was up to something. The last time Slocum had seen him, he had left him frustrated, almost fuming, standing in the middle of the road. There was something different. Something—

He turned and looked back toward the Hornbuckle place, and then he saw the smoke. "Damn," he said, and he started riding hard. By the time he was nearing the gate, he knew that the house was on fire. He raced on through and down the lane. He saw the house in flames. It was too far gone to do anything but watch. He kept riding. Where was Merilee? Where was Morton? He rode closer. They were nowhere in sight. He rode around the burning house and out to the corral. He could find no sign of them, but he did see the clumps of hair on the ground. Merilee's hair. Something had happened here.

"Merilee," he shouted. "Morton."

He got no answer. When he was satisfied that neither one was anywhere around, he started to ride out again. At the gate, he almost headed for town after Glad, but then he thought, Maybe Carl Doaks knows something. He turned and raced for Doaks's place. The ride seemed much longer than it had before, but at last he was there. He saw three horses standing in front of the house, all saddled. He jumped down out of the saddle and rushed through the door, not waiting to be invited. When he came bursting into the room, Carl jumped up and reached for a gun. Then he saw that it was Slocum. Slocum saw the Hornbuckles. They were laid out on Carl's two beds.

"They'll be okay," said Carl.

Slocum went to Merilee's side and looked down at her. Her hair was crudely cropped. She had a black eye, and the rest of her face was bruised and cut. Her eyes were closed, but when she heard Carl talking to someone, she opened them slowly and saw Slocum standing there. "Slocum," she said.

"Don't talk," he said. "Just rest." He glanced at Doaks. "How's Morton?"

"He's beat up, but he'll survive it, too," said Doaks. "I saw the smoke and rode over to investigate. Morton and Merilee were both tied to the corral fence. Beat up bad. Merilee's pants had been jerked down to her knees, and her shirt was all cut up. Her hair was cut up like you see it."

"Did they say—"

"Gordy Glad's the one that done it," said Doaks. "He never gave no reason."

"I know the reason," said Slocum, his jaw set hard.

"That damn drunk Jackson was with him," said Doaks.

"Do we need to take them in to see Doc?" Slocum asked.

"I think they'll be all right," Doaks said. "I don't think nothing's broke. It's mostly their faces, and I doctored them up as best I could."

"Well," said Slocum, "I've got some business in town. I'll see if I can't send Doc out here, just to be on the safe side."

"All right," said Doaks.

Without another word, Slocum walked out the door and climbed back into the saddle. At the road, he turned toward Hard Luck and the Hard Luck Saloon.

15

All the ride into Hard Luck, Slocum was thinking about
how he would kill Gordy Glad. He did not want to simply
blow him to hell. He wanted to make him suffer, more than
Glad had made the Hornbuckles suffer. He tried to think of
ways to do that, but Glad was much too fast to mess around
with. He might not have a choice. Shooting that fast, one
did not always have the option of hitting a man in the arm
or shoulder. But he did not want it to be over with like
that—that fast. Glad had to hurt some. Slocum did not race
into Hard Luck. He took his time, riding leisurely, thinking
as he rode. He could not get the image of Merilee tied to
that damned fence, and the disgusting face of the man who
had done the deed, out of his mind.

As he rode down the main street of Hard Luck, he again
saw Sheriff Hardy standing on the board sidewalk. He
tipped his hat. "Don't worry, Sheriff," he said. "I ain't fixing to bother any Hemps as long as they don't bother me."

"I can't think who's left to bother with," the sheriff mut-
tered as Slocum passed him by.

Luck was with Slocum as he approached the Hard Luck
Saloon. He saw the man Jackson heading toward the front
door. He hauled back on the reins as he hove up alongside

Jackson. "Hey, you, Jackson," he said. Jackson stopped and looked, and saw Slocum. His eyes widened. It was time, he thought. He flew into a fit of choking and coughing, and finally he spat out a great gob of nastiness onto the street. Sucking in a deep breath, he looked up at Slocum with red and watery eyes out of a face which was colored deep purple from the strain.

"There's an overhanging rock on the road into town," Slocum said. "A big dead tree on top of it. Lightning struck. You know the place?"

"I know it," said Jackson.

"Tell your buddy Glad that I'll be there waiting for him."

"He said you was to come into the saloon," Jackson protested.

"It's that or nothing," said Slocum. "You tell him."

Without waiting for a response, he turned the Appaloosa and headed back in the direction from which he had come. Jackson stood for a moment watching him, hesitating. He thought about calling after him, but decided against it. He turned to hurry into the Hard Luck Saloon. Inside, he found Glad seated at a table with his back against the wall. He was sipping from a cup of coffee. Glad looked up as Jackson came coughing up to his table.

"At least turn your goddamned head," he said.

Jackson turned away and finished his hacking. Then he turned back and pulled out a chair. He leaned across the table to speak in low conspiratorial tones. "I just seen him," he said.

"Who?" said Glad.

"Slocum," said Jackson. "Who else? He just rode into town."

"It won't be long then," said Glad.

"Wait a minute," said Jackson. "He seen me, too."

"So?"

"He called out to me, and he said to tell you that he'd be

waiting out on the road for you at the place with the rock hanging over the road. The place with the lightning-struck tree. He said he'd be out there waiting for you. Then he turned around and headed back out of town. Just like that. That's what he said, and that's what he done."

Glad reached into a pocket and took out a bill. He put it on the table and shoved it toward Jackson. "Go get a fresh bottle," he said. "And don't open it."

"Don't open it?" said Jackson.

"You heard me right. Now go get it. And two glasses."

Jackson hurried over to the bar and bought the bottle. He took it and two glasses back to the table where Glad waited. Glad took the bottle and opened it. Then he poured two drinks and shoved one toward Jackson. Jackson downed his in a hurry. Glad picked up his glass and sniffed. He sipped. Finally he drank it down. Then he poured two more.

"So Slocum's going to wait for me out on the road," he said.

"That's what he told me," said Jackson.

"I'll accommodate him. And you'll go with me. I'll need a witness."

"You going to kill him?"

"That's what I came to town for," said Glad. "I'll shoot him right between the eyes."

"Right between the eyes," Jackson repeated, and then he succumbed to another horrible fit of coughing and hacking and choking.

Slocum made it back to the spot in the road he had designated to Jackson. He dismounted and tied the Appaloosa to some small brush beside the road, in plain sight. He moved back into the woods a little and looked around. At last he found a piece of fallen branch just the right size around. He could not quite touch his fingers together when he closed them around it. It was too long, though, so he had to prop one end of it against a rock and stamp on it to break it off. He picked it up and tested it. It was a good size. Just right for gripping and swinging. He climbed up on top of the overhanging rock and looked toward Hard Luck, but he could see no one coming as yet. Glad would be coming along, though. He knew that. He made his way back down to the road and studied the brush all along the edge. There were several large rocks and lots of thick brush, any number of places to hide, but he needed a special spot. One he could get behind and not be seen from the road, yet one he could get out from behind in a big hurry. At last he settled on a small boulder that was sticking up out of the ground. About four feet across, it stood almost shoulder high to Slocum. He stepped behind it to check it out more closely. Because of the way the road curved and the way the brush grew, he could not be seen from the road. He could not see the road ahead either, but he could see it beyond. If someone came along, he would hear them, and as they moved on past him, he would see them. The way around the boulder was clear on his left side. He could get out fast onto the road. He decided to settle there and wait.

It wasn't too many more minutes before he heard the sound of approaching horses' hoofs. Two horses, he thought. They were moving at a good clip. As they approached the overhanging rock, they slowed down. Then Slocum could hear voices, but they did not sound clear to him. He waited. They came closer. "There's his horse," said someone. Slocum thought it sounded like Jackson. In another minute, he was sure, when Jackson began to hack and cough and splutter. The horses came closer. Soon he could tell that they were right across the boulder from him. They were moving past him. Then he saw them. They stopped. Glad was on the left. That put him between Slocum and Jackson. That was good. For a moment they sat silent in their saddles.

"Slocum?" Glad said. "Slocum, where are you?"

"He's hiding," said Jackson.

"Slocum, I come out here for a fair fight with you. I brought along a witness to prove that it's fair. Come on out."

Slocum stepped out from behind the boulder, raised the piece of branch and brought it down hard across the ass of Glad's horse. The animal neighed in surprise and reared. Glad fell back, but he managed to keep his seat. With the horse in a high rear and Glad laid back, his head was just the right height for Slocum's action, and Slocum swung the branch again. This time he caught Glad across the back of the head with a sickening thump. Glad's hands released the reins. The horse came down, then kicked up again, this time with his back legs. Glad, unconscious, fell over the horse's neck, and the horse started to run.

"Catch him up," Slocum shouted to Jackson.

Jackson hesitated but an instant. Then he kicked his own horse and raced after Glad's runaway. Before he could catch it, Glad slipped off the saddle and fell hard to the ground. Slocum followed on foot. Jackson stopped his horse and sat in the saddle coughing. When Slocum reached the fallen gunman, he leaned over and took the two six-guns out of their holsters. Then he tossed them as far as he could into the brush. He looked around on both sides of the road. Then he took hold of Glad's collar and dragged him to the side. There was a flat rock laying there about the size and look of a cow pie, and Slocum placed Glad's right hand carefully on the rock. Then he bashed it with the piece of branch he was still carrying. He smashed it several times. For good measure, he stamped it with his boot heel. He thought that he must have broken every bone in the hand. It was a bruised and bloody mess. He grabbed Glad's collar again and moved him over so he could place the left hand on the rock, and he did the same thing to that one. Jackson had recovered from his latest fit by then and was watching with unbelieving eyes.

Then Slocum rolled Glad onto his face. He adjusted the arms so that they were both at Glad's side, the elbows up. He swung the stick again, landing a sharp blow to the back of the right elbow. He heard it snap. Then he moved to the other side and broke the left elbow. He tossed the stick aside. He reached down and rolled the unconscious man over once more and bent to unfasten his britches. Then he pulled them down to Glad's ankles. Jackson finally found his voice.

"What have you done?" he whined.

"It'll be a long while before he ever uses a gun again," said Slocum. "If he ever gets to where he can pull a gun again, he'll probably pull it on himself." He walked over to where Jackson still sat in his saddle in the middle of the road and held out his hand. "Give me your canteen," he said. Jackson nervously handed Slocum the canteen that had been hanging from his saddle horn. Slocum took it and walked back to where the mangled Glad lay beside the road. He stood over Glad and poured water on his face. Glad sputtered and spat and woke up. He opened his eyes and saw Slocum standing over him. He started to sit up, but when he did, he put pressure on his elbows. He screamed with the pain and lay back down.

"Oh, God," he said. "What have you done to me?"

"You figure it out," said Slocum.

The pain slowly began to course through Glad's body, and he moaned aloud.

"I can't get up," he said.

"I guess I could've just left you tied to a fence," Slocum said, "but that idea's already been took."

"What the hell did you do?"

"I just put you out of business for a spell," said Slocum. "That's all. Oh, yeah. I expect the word'll get around, and when it does, I bet there are a whole lot of folks out there who'll be wanting to take a crack at you. I give you a year at most to live."

"Damn you," snarled Glad. "You son of a bitch. I came out here on purpose to give you a fair fight."

"After what you did to my friends," said Slocum, "I didn't figure you deserved a fair fight. So long now. I expect you'll be getting out of town as soon as you can."

Slocum turned and walked back out on the road. Then he started walking toward where his Appaloosa waited patiently below the overhanging rock. Jackson watched him go. In another moment, he dismounted and hurried over to Glad's side. He knelt beside the onetime gunman and stared at the hands and the elbows. He winced at the sight.

"Well," said Glad. "Do something."

"What can I do?" said Jackson.

"Get me to a doctor."

"Can you get up?" said Jackson.

"You'll have to lift me."

"I . . . I don't think I can."

"You want any more whiskey?" said Glad. "Lift me up."

Jackson shoved his hands under Glad's shoulders and heaved. With Glad helping all he could, they managed to get him to his feet.

"Come on," said Jackson. "I'll help you get on your horse."

They started to move toward the road, but Glad's feet wouldn't move, and he stumbled over the trousers that were still down around his ankles. He screamed with fright as he fell, and with pain when he landed.

"God damn," he said. "What the hell did he do to me?"

"Your britches is down around your ankles," said Jackson.

"Well, get me up again."

Jackson pulled at Glad's coat until he got him to his knees. He pulled harder and uprighted him once again. "What now?" he said.

"Pull my britches up, damn it," said Glad. Jackson walked around to stand in front of Glad. He knelt to reach down for the trousers, but he hesitated when he discovered just what was staring him right in the eyes. "Well, go on," said Glad. "What are you waiting for?"

Jackson deliberately averted his eyes, took hold of the trousers and lifted them up to Glad's waist. He fumbled with the button until he got it fastened. Glad's pecker was hanging loose out of the fly, and Jackson just hoped that with all his pain, Glad would not notice.

"Come on," he said, and he walked Glad to his horse. He managed to keep Glad upright while Glad got a foot in a stirrup. Then he pushed on Glad's back while Glad managed to swing himself into the saddle. The pain was getting worse, and Glad was biting his lip to keep from whimpering out loud.

"You'll have to take the reins," he said.

Jackson took the reins and walked back to his own horse. He mounted up and started a slow ride back to Hard Luck. The ride seemed to have tripled in length. Along the way, Glad's head dropped, his chin resting on his chest. His eyes opened wide. "Jackson," he called out.

"What?"

"My dick's out."

"No one'll see it till we get to Doc's office," Jackson said.

"Oh, damn it," wailed Glad. Now he was not only beaten and battered and crippled, maybe for life, but he was also humiliated. "Why didn't you put it back?"

"I ain't touching that thing," said Jackson. "It would take a whole case of whiskey to get me to touch that thing. Doc'll take care of you. Doc's business makes him touch them things all the time."

Glad wanted to say something else to Jackson, but just then Jackson suffered another attack of coughing and spewing. Glad just moaned as they continued on their way. Several times he thought he would die before they finished the trip, but then he thought that it was hurting too much for him to die. He knew that he would survive the ordeal.

He thought about what Slocum had said. There were people out there who would happily, greedily even, take advantage of his miserable condition to kill him. The bastards. They wouldn't have dared when he was healthy. He wished it would quit hurting. He hoped that no one would be nearby when they reached the doc's place. He couldn't stand the thought of being seen in town with his rod hanging out. He wished that Slocum had just gone ahead and killed him and gotten it all over with. The son of a bitch. The dirty bastard. The asshole.

Doc took Glad's coat and shirt off and flung them on a chair. He grimaced at the look of what Slocum had done. While he was busy examining the wounds, Jackson moved to the chair and rummaged in Glad's pockets for his money. Finding it, he tucked it into his own pocket and slinked out the door.

"How bad is it, Doc?" moaned Glad.

"I don't think you'll be using these for a long spell," Doc said. "Maybe never."

Glad groaned and rolled his head. "They'll kill me," he said.

"Who's they?" said Doc.

"Anyone. Any number of them. But they'll kill me for sure."

Doc moved over to a shelf for a bottle of something and pulled a cork out. He moved back to the table where Glad was laid out.

"This is going to hurt," he said.

"Doc," said Glad, "did you put my dick away?"

16

Slocum rode back to Carl Doaks's place and found the two Hornbuckles still there. Merilee was still in bed, although she was sitting up and staring at the wall. Morton was sitting in a chair at the table sipping from a cup of coffee that Doaks had provided. Slocum took off his hat as he entered the room, hanging it on a peg by the door. He nodded to Morton. "You all right, boy?" he asked.

"I'll be right as rain in just a little while," Morton said.

Slocum moved slowly on over to the bed, and he sat down on the edge beside Merilee. She did not look at him. "Merilee," he said. She did not respond. "Merilee, are you all right?" She turned to face him, and once again, he saw the battered face, the black eye, the cuts and bruises. "It'll all heal," he said.

"All except the humiliation," she said. "And when will he be back? That's the meanest man I ever met up with."

"He won't be back," Slocum said.

"What?"

"He won't be back."

"You killed him?"

"Not right off," said Slocum, "but I fixed him good. He won't be bothering anyone else."

Morton came up out of his chair. "What'd you do, Slocum?" he said. "What'd you do to the son of a bitch?"

"Watch your goddamn language, Morton," said Merilee. Then she looked back at Slocum. "What did you do to the son of a bitch?" she asked.

Slocum thought about how he would respond. He did not like bragging about his deeds to anyone, but these two deserved to know the fate of the bastard who had assaulted them and burned their house to the ground. "Well," he said, "first of all I knocked him silly with a big stick. Then while he was out cold, I smashed every bone in each of his hands."

"God," said Morton.

Carl Doaks stared at Slocum in disbelief.

"Somebody'll kill him, won't they, Slocum?" said Merilee. "But first of all, he'll have to worry about it for a while."

"That's what I figured," said Slocum. "Oh, yeah. I broke both his elbows."

"Lord God," said Morton. "Is that all?"

"Ain't it enough?" Slocum said.

"Well, sure, but—"

"I did take his britches down to his ankles. Left him beside the road like that."

Merilee burst into laughter. Then she was joined by Morton and Carl Doaks. At last, Slocum laughed with them.

"Hey," said Merilee. "With his hands and his arms all mashed up like that, how will he ever get them back up?"

"He had his little hacking man named Jackson with him, for a witness, he said. I reckon Jackson will have to pull up his pants for him."

They all laughed some more. Merilee swung her legs over the edge of the bed and sat up beside Slocum. "You couldn't have brought me any better medicine," she said. "Slocum?"

"What?"

"I want to go to town and see the son of a bitch."

"Me, too," said Morton.

Slocum looked over at Doaks. "What do you think, Carl?" he asked.

Doaks gave a shrug. "I can't see no harm in it," he said.

Doc at last finished wrapping and taping and plastering the hands and arms of Gordy Glad. He had also poured Glad full of laudanum, so that the pain was not nearly so bad as it had been. At last Glad sat up on the edge of the table, with a little help from Doc. He felt a little dizzy, so he just sat there for a few moments. Then his head seemed to clear, and he stood up. He asked Doc what he owed him, and Doc told him. "My money's in my coat over there," he said, nodding toward the coat where it had been tossed on a chair. Doc walked over to the chair and picked up the coat. He felt in all of the pockets. Then he looked at Glad.

"There's nothing here," he said.

"What? Nothing?"

"Not a damn thing," said Doc. "I'd say feel for yourself but, well, you know how it is."

"But I had near five hundred dollars," said Glad. "Wait a minute. Jackson. That little runt bastard."

"Well, he did bring you in here," said Doc, "and when I got you on the table, I was too busy to keep an eye on him."

Glad walked down to the sheriff's office and kicked on the door. He yelled, "Open up."

Sheriff Hardy, sitting behind his desk, called back, "It's open. Come on in."

"I can't open the goddamned thing," shouted Glad.

Hardy got up from his chair with a groan of displeasure and walked around the desk to the door. He opened it and stared at Glad, standing there with both arms in slings and both hands wrapped up. "What the hell happened to you?" he said.

"Slocum," said Glad, "but that ain't why I come to see you."

"What for then?"

"That little fucker, Jackson, robbed me. While I was laid out on Doc's table, he went through my coat pockets and stole all my money. Near five hundred."

"How do you know that?" asked Hardy.

"He was the only one there. He's the one took me to the doc. Doc took off my coat and tossed it on a chair. He didn't watch Jackson, but Jackson left, and when I went to pay Doc, there was no money in my pockets. It had to be him."

"If Jackson's got money," said Hardy, "he'll be in the Hard Luck Saloon." He walked to the hat rack and took off his hat. "I'll find him."

"I'm going with you," said Glad.

Sure enough, they found Jackson at the bar in the saloon having a drink. When he saw them coming at him, he flew into a fit of hacking.

"You little son of a bitch," said Glad.

"Just hold on," said Hardy. The two of them waited for Jackson to survive his attack. Then Hardy said, "Jackson, you got any cash on you?"

"Cash?" said Jackson.

"You heard me right. Answer the question."

"I ain't got no money, Sheriff. You know me. Where would I get any money?"

"He pulled out a wad of bills just a while ago, Sheriff," said the barkeep. "Paid me with a twenty. Check that pocket right there." He pointed to the pocket on the outside, top left of Jackson's dirty and wrinkled old coat. Hardy reached for the pocket. Jackson tried to back away, and he put a hand to the pocket to protect it.

"You can't just go and search me like that, can you?" he said.

"Be still, Jackson," said Hardy. He shoved his hand

down into the pocket and came up with the money. Counting it out on the bar, he had nearly five hundred dollars. He looked at Jackson with a snarl on his face. "Like you said, Jackson. I know you. Where the hell did you get this?"

"I—"

"He stole it from me," said Glad.

"Well, I was working for him," Jackson said. "He wasn't in no position to take care of me, so I just took it. That's all. My pay."

"I was buying him a bottle of whiskey a day to follow me around and be a witness," said Glad. "That's all."

Hardy picked the money up off of the bar and held it in front of Jackson's nose. "You could buy an awful lot of whiskey with this," he said. "Likely enough to kill you." He turned and tucked the money into one of Glad's pockets. "I don't know how you'll ever get your hands on it again," he said, "but there it is. You want to press charges against this little shit?"

"No. Never mind," said Glad. "I just wish I had even one good hand. I'd pay him all right."

Jackson started hacking again, and Hardy and Glad headed for the door. Just as Glad was about to walk out, Jackson recovered. He called out, "Hey. Gordy. Buy me a bottle?"

Out on the sidewalk, Sheriff Hardy suddenly turned on Glad. "I asked you once before what happened to you. You just said, 'Slocum.' I'll ask again. What the hell happened?"

Just then Slocum, Carl Doaks, Merilee and Morton came riding into town, and Sheriff Hardy looked up and saw them. He waved them over. He had no need, because Merilee and Morton both saw Glad, and he was the reason they had come to town. They rode over and dismounted. Merilee walked right up to Glad and laughed in his face. "You ain't so tough now," she said.

"Leave me alone," said Glad.

"You didn't leave me alone, did you?"

"Nor me," said Morton. "By God, you got just what the hell was coming to you. There is some justice in this world."

"Sheriff," said Glad, "do I have to stand here and take this shit?"

"All of you shut up," said Hardy. "Come on over to my office."

They all followed Hardy back to his office and went inside. Glad sat in a chair. Hardy sat behind his desk. The rest stood. "All right now," said Hardy. "I want the whole story, and I want it now."

Everyone was silent until Merilee said, "Who do you want it from?"

"Whoever can start at the beginning."

Merilee proceeded to tell Hardy how Glad had come to their ranch and what he had done. All the time she was talking, Hardy was staring at her face. When she had finished her tale, he looked over at Morton. Then he looked at Glad.

"Is that all true?" he said. "Did you do that?"

"Hell," said Glad, "I didn't hurt them none. I just wanted to get Slocum mad enough to fight me."

"It worked, too, didn't it?" said Morton, grinning.

"All right. That's enough," said Hardy. "What next?"

Carl Doaks jumped in, telling about how he had seen the smoke and rushed over to investigate. He told how he had found the Hornbuckles, rescued them and taken them over to his house. "Glad was already gone," he concluded.

"Then Slocum showed up," said Merilee.

"There at Doaks's place?" said Hardy.

"That's right," said Doaks. "We told him what had happened, and he took off."

Hardy looked at Slocum. "Where'd you go?" he demanded.

"Rode into town," said Slocum. "I found Jackson and told him to tell this asshole here that I'd meet him out on the road to fight it out. Then I went back out to wait. He finally come along. I knew he would. He'd been trying to get me to fight with him. I reckon he was looking for a gunfight, but that ain't what he got. I whipped him up good. That's all there is to it. That's the whole story."

Hardy leaned back in his chair and scratched his head. "Does anyone want to press any charges against anyone?" he asked. No one said anything. "All right," Hardy said, "you can all go. I'd be just as glad if I never saw any of you again."

"You'll see me again," said Slocum as he moved to the door.

Out on the sidewalk, Merilee stepped into Glad's path. "It sure does my heart good to see you like this," she said. "The only thing that could have been better would be if I'd seen you laying out there beside the road with your britches down. I bet you was a sight."

"I ain't never got a kick out of seeing anybody hurt before," said Morton, "but I sure do like this. Slocum fixed you up good and proper."

Glad stomped his way around Merilee and was moving down the street toward the hotel. Carl Doaks shouted after him, "How many men you killed, Glad? How many of them had brothers? Fathers? Sons? Good friends? How long will it be before one of them shows up to kill you? Huh?"

Down at the Hard Luck Saloon, Jackson finished the drink he'd had in front of him on the bar when he had been so rudely interrupted by the sheriff and Gordy Glad. Then he looked around the room. There were several customers in the place. "Somebody buy me a drink?" he said. No one answered. "I bought a round a while ago," he said. "You was all in here. I bought everyone in here a drink. Won't one of you buy me one? Just one? I need another drink real bad."

"Get out of here, Jackson," said the barkeep.

"Wait a minute," said Jackson. "You seen me buy a round for the house. Before the sheriff come in. You seen me. You took my money."

"Turns out it wasn't your money," said the barkeep. "You stole it from that poor crippled up bastard who couldn't defend himself. Ain't nobody going to buy you a drink now, so get on out of here."

"Now wait a minute—"

Just then a cowboy sitting at a nearby table got up and moved to the bar to stand behind Jackson. He grabbed the collar of Jackson's coat from behind, and grabbed a handful of the seat of Jackson's trousers. Then half lifting the little man, he walked him to the door and pitched him through the batwings. Jackson flew out into the street, landing on his face and sliding a ways. He managed to sit up and rub his face, and when he brought away his hand, he saw that there was blood on it. He turned his head to look back into the saloon, intending to shout some nasty names at the bartender and at the customers in there. Instead he started to cough. He coughed a string of coughs so fast and furious that he could not catch his breath. He thought he was going to die right there in the street. He had to get a breath to keep living, and he could not get one. He just kept coughing. He did not want it to end like this out in front of everyone in town. At last, though, he hacked up a horrible wad and spat it out. Well, mostly. Some of it dribbled down his chin. He sat there gasping for breath. He could feel tears running down his face. It seemed to be over with for the time being. He still sat there, though, breathing as deeply as he could. Then four horses came walking down the street right toward him. He put an arm up in front of his face and tried to pull his head into his shoulder like a turtle going into its shell. The horses stopped walking. He lowered his arm and squinted up to see Merilee sitting on her horse standing right beside him. He whimpered. Merilee hawked and spat right in his face.

"You piece of rat shit," she said. She kicked her horse in the sides and moved on toward the edge of town along with her brother, Doaks and Slocum.

17

Elihu Hemp called another family meeting. When everyone was gathered, he looked over his crippled crew with profound sadness in his heart. There was Ezra with his shot ass, Micah with his two useless arms, and now Ferdie with only one leg. Asa and Eben were dead and buried. He still had a few healthy family members, brothers and cousins, but the ranks were thinning seriously. He sat behind his big desk in silence, and the rest of the room kept quiet as well. They knew that Elihu had some serious business to talk over with them. At last, old Elihu looked up. His gaze roved around the room, looking at each face, the healthy and the crippled.

"I've just received some disturbing news," he said finally. "Jackson, the town drunk, came out here to tell me about it. You know I hired that man Glad to take care of Slocum for us. Well, it seems that Slocum has put Glad out of commission. Smashed both of his hands and broke both of his elbows. We're back where we started. We're where we started except that we have two dead and three crippled. Slocum's too much for us. We have to quit."

"Elihu," said Ferdie, still doped up on laudanum, "you mean we ain't going to get even with him for what he's did to us? Me with only one leg left. Everyone will laugh at us behind our back."

"We'll just have to live with it," Elihu said. "Every time we tried to even the score with Slocum, he just got that much more ahead of us. It has to stop here. No more trying to get even with Slocum. No more harassing the Hornbuckles. We're through with all that."

"We have to eat crow?" said Micah.

"And like it," said Elihu. "Eat it and like it."

Jackson had a little cash in his pockets again. Old Elihu Hemp had paid him for the information regarding Gordy Glad, so he was back in the Hard Luck Saloon. Brace the bartender allowed him in, in spite of his better judgment. Jackson bought a bottle and sat down at a table with it. He was there hacking and coughing. Brace wished the little bastard would just go ahead and die. Jackson, on the other hand, was thrilled to have a little money again, but he was also worried that he might not get hold of any more for some time. Maybe never. He resented the hell out of what Sheriff Hardy had done to him, taking away all that money he had gotten from that sorry ex-gunfighter Gordy Glad. Gordy couldn't have done anything to him. Hell, Gordy couldn't even pull his own pants up. Or take them down. Suddenly Jackson wondered how Gordy was managing to do his business in the outhouse. It was a hell of a problem. How would anyone with no arms get along in this world? Why, the son of a bitch couldn't even kill himself unless he climbed up on a big cliff and jumped off, and Jackson couldn't think of any place nearby that was high enough for that. He hacked and spat, and Brace the bartender shouted at him.

"Jackson, if you spit on my floor again, I'll toss your ass out of here for good. You hear me? I mean for good."

"All right, all right. I hear you," said Jackson, and he coughed some more. He did not spit, though. He was getting an idea. He could go back to work for Glad. Glad would not have much choice. He needed a pair of hands to take care of him. Jackson would go see him and make him that offer. He would take care of the killer in exchange for the killer taking care of him again financially. Glad might not like it very well, but the way Jackson looked at it, the man would have to go for it. Who else would undress him at night and dress him again the next morning? Who else would take the son of a bitch to the outhouse? Who would reach into his pocket for money to pay for his meals and drinks and such? Having figured that out, Jackson perked up considerably. Of course, just then, he had a bottle of whiskey and no desire to go to work. He would let Glad suffer through the night alone and approach him in the morning. By then, not having eaten, drank, shat or pissed, Glad would likely accept any offer that Jackson had to make.

Merilee Hornbuckle was in much better spirits after seeing what Slocum had done to Gordy Glad. She kept thinking about the no-good son of a bitch laying in the ditch beside the road, his hands smashed, his elbows broken and his pants down around his ankles. She tried to imagine just what he had to do now to even survive. Would someone with an old grudge show up and kill him, or would he just starve to death laying in his own mess? She took delight in these thoughts. Morton was much better. He and Slocum went out riding the range, checking on the cattle, checking the fences. They ran into Carl Doaks and worked with him some. It seemed that the Hemps had backed off. There was no trouble anymore. Things were looking good all around.

It was the morning of Slocum's eighth day. Merilee had fixed a big breakfast at Carl Doaks's house, and they had all eaten their fill and washed it down with numerous cups of coffee. Then Doaks, Morton and Slocum had ridden out. Merilee finished cleaning up after the meal and was thinking about what to do next when she heard a rider coming up. Instinctively, she grabbed a rifle and went to the door. It was Carl Doaks come back. She put the rifle down and stepped aside to let him in. Doaks took off his hat as he entered the house.

"Hi, Carl," Merilee said. "You come back in a hurry."

"Yeah," said Carl. "There ain't really all that much to do out there. Slocum and Morton will manage all right. I didn't ask you this morning, how are you feeling?"

"I'm all right, Carl. Seeing that bastard in town, the shape he was in, it was like real good medicine."

"Yeah. Well, I'm glad you're feeling better."

"Sit down," she said. "Can I pour you a cup of coffee?"

"Thanks," he said. "I probably had enough already, but that sounds good."

Merilee poured two cups of coffee and sat down at the table with Doaks. Doaks took a sip of his. "Your coffee is a whole lot better than mine," he said.

"I can show you how I fix it," she said.

"That's all right. I'd just as soon drink yours."

"Did you come back just to see me?" she said.

"Well, I came back to—well, to see how you was feeling."

"Is that all? You seen me this morning. I fixed a meal for you."

"I know but, well, there was someone else around, and I . . . I think about you a lot. I get lonesome for—well, not for other men. You know, it makes me feel good having you around here."

"Carl?"

"Yes?"

"About me and Slocum—"

"You don't have to talk about that," he said.

"But I want to. That one time, it just happened. There's nothing between me and Slocum. When he's got his money for killing Asa Hemp, he'll ride on. I knew that all along. It's just that, well, women have needs the same as men. Me

and him was here alone. It happened. I ain't going to apologize for it. I ain't sorry for it. I just wanted you to know
the way things are."

Carl Doaks stared at his coffee cup. Clearly, he was embarrassed. His face was a little flushed. He couldn't think
of anything to say. At last, he lifted his cup for another sip
of coffee.

"It ain't like I was a virgin, Carl," she said. "You know I
was a married woman once."

"I know it, Merilee," he said. "And I don't mind. Not really. It just ain't none of my business. That's all. I'm kind
of glad that, like you said, there ain't nothing between the
two of you. I'm glad of that."

"Why, Carl?"

"Well, because I . . . I like you, Merilee."

She stood up and paced to the coffeepot on the stove-
top. She picked it up and topped off her cup. Then she
poured a little into Doaks's cup. She walked back to the
stove and replaced the pot. "Well," she said, "I'm glad you
like me."

Doaks sensed that he was not doing so well with this
conversation. He had already let way too much time go by,
keeping his mouth shut, keeping his feelings to himself. If
anyone was to blame for what happened between Merilee
and Slocum, it was he himself. "It's more than that, Merilee," he said. Then he ducked his head again. Merilee
moved back to the table and sat down facing him.

"Tell me, Carl," she said.

"It's way more than that. I like your brother. Hell, I even
like Slocum. But with you, well, I like you a lot. I . . . I love
you, Merilee."

"I never thought I'd hear you say them words."

"It was hard for me to say. I've wanted to say them to
you for a long time, but I just couldn't get it out. I'm a
blockhead. I ain't never spent much time around women.
Sometimes I hate myself for being so slow-witted."

"I don't think you're slow-witted at all, Carl," she said. "In fact, I love you, too."

Doaks looked up into her face, black eye and all. "You do?" he said.

"Yes. I do."

"Well, Merilee, would you— I mean, will you marry up with me?"

"I'd be proud to, Carl," she said.

"Oh, I . . . I don't know what to say."

"You don't need to say nothing now. You've said it all."

"I can say that I ain't never been this happy before, not in my whole life."

"Me, too, Carl." She stood up and walked around the table to stand beside him. He turned and looked up into her face. She took hold of his arm and gently pulled him to his feet, and when he was standing there in front of her, she reached up and put her arms around his neck. He wasn't going to be too slow this time. He leaned over slightly to kiss her on the mouth. Softly. Gently. She slipped a hand up onto the back of his head and pressed it firmly, kissing him harder, opening her lips, and he responded.

Out on the range, Slocum came across a cow with a broken horn. She needed doctoring to keep infection out of the break. He told Morton, and they decided to ride back to the house to see if Doaks had the stuff they would need to do the job.

"If he ain't got it," Slocum said, "we'll have to ride to town for it."

"We had some at our place," said Morton, "but it's gone. Like everything else."

"Water under the bridge," Slocum said.

Riding back to the house, Morton did his best not to stare at Slocum. He kept thinking about all that Slocum had done for them. Mostly he thought about the spectacle of Gordy Glad in town with both arms wrapped up tight.

He thought, also, about what Glad had done to him and mostly what he had done to Merilee, and that made him feel even better about what Slocum had done. He had wanted to see Glad dead, but it was even better the way Slocum had done it. When they reached the ranch house, Slocum rode directly to the corral, where the horses could drink from the trough there. He was a little ahead of Morton, and he walked on to the house. He had seen Doaks's horse at the corral, so he knew that he would be inside to be asked about the medicine for the cow. As he walked up to the house, he came up along one side. He happened to glance in the window, and he saw Merilee and Doaks in bed, both naked as jaybirds. He turned quickly to head off Morton, who was coming along behind him. He grabbed Morton by the shoulders.

"Let's go to town for that medicine," he said.

"But Carl might have some of it in the house."

"Carl and Merilee don't need to be bothered just now," said Slocum. "Let's go."

Morton started to protest again, but then his eyes lit up with understanding, and a smile spread across his face. "Oh," he said. "I get it."

"Shut up," said Slocum. "Let's go to town."

They walked back to their horses and mounted up, turning them to ride into Hard Luck. Morton was still grinning as they turned onto the road.

Inside the house, Doaks was laying on top of Merilee between her widespread legs. He was gently moving in and out, slowly pumping his rod into her wet slit. She moved rhythmically with him, their two bodies working together like a well-oiled machine. Merilee's arms were around Carl, and she was moaning softly and lowly.

"Oh, Carl," she said. "I love it. I love it."

"Me, too," said Carl. "Oh, yeah."

"Come on now," she said. "Go faster."

Carl humped faster than before, picking up speed.

"Oh, yes," she said. "Faster. Harder."

Carl's motions grew furious and desperate. He pounded in and out. His loins slapped against hers loudly, and they could both hear the squishing sound as his cock went in and out.

"Oh," she said. "Fuck me, Carl. Fuck me."

"Oh, yes," he cried out. "Yes. I will. I am."

He drove in and out more desperately than ever. All of a sudden her hands slid down his back to his buttocks. She gripped one cheek with each hand and pressed him down, stopping his movements with his tool deep inside her.

"Wait," she said. "Let me turn over."

He backed reluctantly out of her and moved over, allowing her to turn onto her belly. She snaked up onto her hands and knees, and Carl could see her gorgeous ass poking out toward him. He could see the wet patch of wondrousness he had already been probing. He moved behind her and shoved his rod into her wet slit once again. The sensation was marvelous for both of them. He drove in and out. She rocked her rear end to the same rhythm. Carl suddenly felt the pressure in his balls building up like a volcano about to erupt.

"Oh," he said. "Oh. Oh. Oh."

Merilee knew that he was about to come, but she was not yet ready for it to end. She stopped arching her buttocks into him. She moved forward causing him to slip out. "Oh," he said. She turned and rolled him over onto his back. His throbbing rod was pointed to the ceiling. Merilee looked at it and smiled. She took hold of it and then swung astraddle of him, guiding the tool back into the place where it belonged, settling down on it, allowing it to slide deeply back inside her. She sat down heavily on Carl's middle, his tool as far into her as it could go, and then she began to slide back and forth. Slowly at first, then more quickly, then faster and faster. Sweat dripped off of her body down onto Carl's chest. He gasped for breath. Merilee groaned. Her groans became almost wild cries as she rocked back and forth with fury. At last, she thought that she could take no more. She was done for. She fell forward onto his chest, and the sweat of their two bodies mingled. She kissed him hungrily on the mouth, just as he began to thrust upward fast and desperate, and then he burst forth.

"Ahhhh," he cried out.

She lay heavily on top of him, both of them exhausted. Gradually his rod relaxed, and soon it slipped out of its comfortable hole. He could feel the juices of both of their bodies running down and soaking him. His nostrils were filled with her scent, the love juices, the sweat—all of it. He stroked her back and her butt with both his hands. At last she rolled off of him to lay beside him, smiling contentedly.

"Merilee," he said.

"What, Carl?"

"Let's go to town and get married. Right away. Right now."

"I've got a lot of getting ready to do," she said. "Let's go in and do it tomorrow."

18

On the morning of Slocum's ninth day, Slocum rode into Hard Luck with Merilee, Carl Doaks and Morton. They went straight to the home of the preacher, where Merilee and Doaks were married in a simple ceremony. Slocum congratulated both of the newlyweds heartily. Morton was extremely pleased with the union. The couple, along with the bride's younger brother, would live at Doaks's place. The combining of the two herds, which had been done earlier, was now a fixed deal. When the wedding ceremony was over and done, the four of them went to the eating place for a big, celebratory breakfast. Everyone was happy. Gordy Glad and the lion's share of the Hemps were debilitated. Everything seemed to be looking up. Slocum would get his money the next day and be on his way. When they had finished eating and left the joint, Slocum said, "Morton, let's you and me stay in town for a little while. I've got some things I want to do, and I could use some company."

Morton gave Slocum a knowing look with a sly grin, and said, "Sure, Pard. I'll hang around a spell with you."

Carl and Merilee looked at each other and smiled. Merilee said, "Can we expect you back about lunchtime?"

"Well, yeah," said Slocum. "We might make it back by then."

"We'll be counting on it," said Merilee.

Merilee and Carl climbed on their horses and headed for the ranch, leaving Slocum and Morton standing on the sidewalk. The two footloose cowhands watched them ride off. At last Morton said, "What are we going to do, Slocum?"

"Hell," said Slocum. "I don't know."

"You said you had some things you wanted to take care of."

"I just thought we'd ought to let them two alone for a spell," Slocum said. "That's all."

"There's always the saloon," said Morton.

"It's a little early for drinking, ain't it?" Slocum answered. "Let's just stroll down the sidewalk here."

"Okay."

Up in his hotel room, Gordy Glad lay on top of the covers of the bed, fully dressed. He had been like that all night long. He was beginning to feel desperate. He had no idea what he was going to do. He was alone and helpless. He thought about getting up and going back over to Doc Grubbs's office. The doc would help him. Doctors were in business to help people. Yes, he decided. That's what he would do. He struggled to get up onto his feet. His door stood open as he had no way to close it, and if he had closed it, there was no way he could open it again. He was about to walk out of the room when he heard the all too familiar sound of Jackson's whooping. He waited. In another minute, Jackson poked his head into the room.

"Howdy, Mr. Glad," he said.

"What do you want here, Jackson?" Glad said.

"I got to thinking about you, the shape you're in and all," Jackson said. "It come to me that you might be in need of some help, and me being out of a job, so to speak, I thought I'd come and check up on you."

Glad wanted to call Jackson a sleazy little worm of a bastard, but he thought better of it. "I do need some help," he said. "Come in."

Sheriff Hardy was sitting in a chair on the sidewalk in front of his office when the stranger rode into town. He was a man with a hard look, and he was riding well armed. He had a Winchester rifle in a saddle boot, and Hardy could easily make out two six-guns at the man's waist. He wore a black suit and a black flat-brimmed hat. He sported a drooping mustache, and he was red in the face. Hardy thought that the man looked like trouble riding in, and just when all the recent trouble seemed to be over with. He thought about flagging the man down and having a talk with him, but he decided against it. He had never seen the man before, yet he thought there was something familiar about him. He decided that it was just the common look of a gunfighter. Well, he would wait and see what happened. The man might be just riding through.

Slocum and Morton were walking down the street, and they, too, spotted the stranger. They stopped walking and watched him ride by, down to the saloon. He stopped, dismounted, tied his horse and walked in through the batwing doors. "He looks like a tough one," said Morton.

"Yeah," Slocum agreed. "Have you seen him around here before?"

"No," said Morton. "Never."

"He's got a familiar look about him," said Slocum. "He looks to me like he might be one of them Hemps."

"Now that you mention it," said Morton, "he does have that look about him."

"Well," said Slocum, "it might just be our imaginations working too hard for our good."

Inside the Hard Luck Saloon, the stranger went straight to the bar. He was the only customer in the place. Brace the barkeep came right over to serve him. "What can I do for you?" he said.

"Shot of whiskey," the man said.

Brace put a glass on the counter and poured it full. The man paid him. "Can you tell me how to get to the Hemp ranch?" he said.

"Sure," said Brace. "Just ride straight out this road." He pointed the man in the right direction. "When you come to it, you'll see a sign over the gate with the Hemp name on it. You can't miss it."

"Thanks," said the stranger. He downed the drink and walked back outside, mounted his horse and turned it in the direction of the ranch. He rode calmly and slowly out of town. On the sidewalk, Hardy watched him go. He hoped that he was gone for good.

Elihu Hemp had sent all the ranch hands out to do their chores. He had given them all specific instructions. Some of the ranch work had been ignored lately, and he had decided that it was high time they all got serious about it again. He was still feeling down about his defeat at the hands of that Slocum, but he had decided that he did not really need the Hornbuckle spread, and he guessed that his kinfolk did not really need avenging. After all, they had all gone looking for trouble. They had gotten what they deserved. He sat on a couch in his sumptuous living room. He was puffing a cigar. An empty coffee cup sat on a nearby table. Emilie walked into the room carrying a pot. "Would you like a little more coffee, dear?" she asked.

Elihu grunted, and Emilie poured his cup full. She put the pot down on the table and sat beside her husband, putting an arm around his shoulders. "Are you feeling all right?" she said.

"Yes," he said. "Yes, I'm all right."

"You don't sound like it," she said. "And you don't look like it. I'm not used to seeing you mope around like this."

"I'll get over it," he said. "It's just all that unpleasant business we've just gone through. Everything's all right. Really."

She leaned over and kissed him on the cheek. "I hope so," she said. "Is there anything I can do for you?"

"No," he said. "You've done more than enough. Emilie, you're the one joy of my life. Have I told you that recently?"

"It has been a little while," she said, "but I think I knew how you felt."

There was a knock at the door, and Emilie got up to answer it. She found herself facing a stranger.

"Yes?" she said.

"I come to see Elihu," the stranger said. "I'm his cousin Lonzo."

"Lonzo?" said Emilie. "We've never met, have we?"

"No, ma'am. I ain't seen Elihu in years."

"Well, come in," she said. "I'm Emilie. Elihu is my husband. Come in. He's right here."

Lonzo Hemp followed Emilie into the living room. She shut the door behind them, and walked across the room toward Elihu. When Elihu saw who his visitor was, he stood up. His face reflected surprise. "Lonzo?" he said. "Is that you?"

"Howdy, Elihu," said Lonzo, extending his hand.

Elihu took the hand and pumped it, a broad smile spreading across his face. "Lonzo, sit down. Make yourself comfortable. My God, how long has it been?"

"We was just kids."

"Yes. Yes. Emilie, this is my cousin, Lonzo."

"I know," she said. "We met at the door."

"Why don't you fetch Cousin Lonzo a cup of coffee?"

"Of course," said Emilie. "Cream or sugar?"

"Just black, ma'am," said Lonzo.

"Please call me Emilie," she said. "I'll be right back."

Emilie walked into the kitchen, and Elihu stared at his long-lost cousin, still with near disbelief. "I can't get over it, Lonzo," he said. "Why, I'd just about given up on ever seeing you again. Where have you been all this time?"

"Up in Montana, Wyoming. Hell, I been all over the West," Lonzo said.

"I'll be," said Elihu. "Well, the important thing is you're here now. I'm sure glad of that."

Emilie came back with a coffee cup and poured it full, then handed it to Lonzo. He thanked her, and she excused herself and took the pot back to the kitchen. Lonzo sipped his coffee. "I didn't come here just for a visit, Elihu," he said.

"Oh?"

"I heard about the trouble you was having down here."

"Oh," said Elihu. "Well, I'm afraid it's all over with. I was after the spread right next to mine, but this fellow Slocum showed up. I guess he spotted Asa and knew him for a wanted man. Killed him for the reward. Then Eben went for Slocum, and Slocum killed him. He shot up Ezra and Micah, and he crippled Ferdie with a landslide. Ferdie's lost a log. I'm whipped, Lonzo. I've give it up."

"Elihu," said Lonzo, "the Hemps is never whipped, and they never give up. That's what I'm here for."

"Lonzo," said Elihu, "I don't want any help. I don't want any more of my family hurt or killed by this Slocum. I've had it. You're welcome here for as long as you want to stay. Why, I'm even shorthanded now with what all Slocum has done to us. I could use another hand. I'd be glad to have you. But I don't want you going after Slocum."

"There ain't nothing you can do about it, Elihu. That's what I come for, and that's my firm intention. It's a matter of family pride. Family honor."

"Lonzo—"

"Listen to me. I've heard about this Slocum. He's got a pretty damn good reputation. He's fast and he's accurate. I've heard plenty about him. But I can take care of him. I don't always fight fair, Cousin. And I always get my man. I ain't never failed yet."

Jackson took Glad to the outhouse and saw to all his needs. Then he took him by Doc's place for another bottle of laudanum. After that, they went to the eating place, where they ordered meals, and Jackson spoon-fed Glad. Glad was humiliated by all this, especially out in public, but there was nothing he could do but take it. Then they walked to the saloon, where they bought a bottle of whiskey. Jackson took the bottle and two glasses to a table and poured two drinks. He had to hold Glad's glass to his lips to allow him to drink. Now and then Jackson had a coughing spell, and Glad had to grit his teeth. He wished that he had someone else to assist him, but Jackson was available. He had to take what he could get. Maybe he could survive it long enough for his arms and hands to heal. Maybe he could get back his old skill. Maybe if he was patient long enough, he would get a chance to even the score with Slocum. That thought kept him going.

Following their noon meal, Slocum and Morton and Carl Doaks rounded up their herd and drove it in to the corral. They built a small fire and stuck the branding iron in it. Then they began roping the young calves that were ready for branding. It would take them most of the afternoon. It was hot work, and they kept at it with no breaks. Morton got himself jerked out of the saddle one time, and kicked up a dust storm when he hit the ground. Slocum caught up the calf that had done the deed, and Carl ran over to Morton's side.

"Are you hurt?" he said.

"Hell, no," said Morton, standing up and dusting himself off. "Just embarrassed is all."

They finished the branding in time for supper, and all three of them were more than ready for the meal. They ate

heartily, and then they started filling up the tub for bathing.
Merilee got first shot at it. They put up a screen for privacy.
When she was done, Carl got his bath, then Morton, and finally Slocum. All of them dressed in clean clothes, and
they sat around sipping fresh coffee. Slocum and Morton
both figured that they would sleep outside that night. The
next morning, they would start building an extra room onto
the house.

Glad had Jackson saddle two horses and ride with him out
of town. When they reached the place where Slocum had
attacked him, the place with the overhanging rock, Glad
sat in the saddle and looked around. "It was right about
here," he said.

"That's how I remember it," said Jackson. "He took
them both and throwed them out that way."

"Go on and see if you can find them," said Glad.

Jackson dismounted and walked into the brush at the
side of the road. He moved slowly, pushing aside brush and
looking on the ground.

"See anything?" called Glad.

"Not yet," said Jackson. He had to pause in his search,
for a hacking fit. When it finally subsided, he continued.
Glad sat in his saddle thinking that the very next fit could
be the one that would kill Jackson. Then he would be left
alone again. He hoped that Jackson would survive for a
while yet. Jackson parted some brush and squinted down at
the ground. He spied something shiny. He reached down
and gripped the handle of a Colt revolver.

"I got one of them," he shouted, and he held it up high
for Glad to see.

"Good," said Glad. "Good. Keep looking." He was
wearing his gunbelt, the holsters empty since Slocum had
tossed away his six-shooters. He would not be able to use
them, of course, but he hated the empty holsters. And the
guns were expensive. Even if he could never use them

again, he would be able to sell them if he became destitute. Over in the brush Jackson had another fit. Glad heaved a sigh. Ten more minutes went by before Jackson finally found the other gun. He came running back to the horses waving them both in the air.

"Be careful," Glad said. "They're both loaded."

Jackson stopped in his tracks and took his fingers off of the triggers. "Oh, yeah," he said.

"Stick them down in my holsters," said Glad. Jackson put the guns in the holsters.

"Now?" he said.

"Let's go back to town," said Glad. He felt some better with his guns back on his hips, even though he could not draw them out.

19

The next morning, Slocum's ninth day, Sheriff Hardy paid a visit to the Doaks place. Although no one was thrilled to see the sheriff, they invited him in and offered him a cup of coffee, which he accepted. He sat down at the table. Merilee continued puttering about as if no one was there. Carl, Slocum and Morton all sat down at the table with Hardy. Slocum and Carl each had another cup of coffee. Finally, Hardy decided to break the ice.

"You folks haven't had any more trouble out here, have you?" he asked.

"Things've been pretty quiet," said Carl. "How come you to ask?"

"Oh, I'm just checking around. I like to keep up with how things're going in my county."

"Anytime we went in and told you what was going on," said Merilee over her shoulder, "you never done nothing about it."

"I never could find any proof," said Hardy. "I investigated. And I do have a hearing scheduled for Ezra this afternoon."

"Already?" said Morton.

"I've informed Elihu, and he's promised to bring Ezra in. The circuit judge got into town last night."

"Well, I'll be damned," said Carl.

"I'm counting on you folks to be there as witnesses."

"We'll be there," said Carl. "What time?"

"One o'clock," said Hardy.

"We'll be there."

"The judge'll just slap his hands," said Merilee. "I think it's a waste of time."

"You ought to have Ferdie in there, too," said Morton, "for chasing Slocum on our range and trying to kill him."

"Swear out a complaint, and I will," said Hardy.

"I heard he lost a leg," said Slocum. "I think that's punishment enough."

"Suit yourself," said the sheriff. "Anyway, I think your troubles are all over. When I talked to Elihu, he said that he was through. He's lost too many of his kin, and good ranch hands at the same time. He told me he was whipped. And you crippled up that gunfighter that was after you. I figure Elihu hired him. Course, I got no proof of that."

"Same old story," Merilee said.

Hardy chose to ignore her. "I been thinking of calling you the Crippler," he said to Slocum. "You've crippled up several good men around here lately."

"We could argue over that word 'good,'" Slocum said.

"Well," said Hardy, standing up, "I'll leave you folks alone now. I just stopped by to tell you about the hearing this afternoon. See you in town then."

It seemed like the whole town was out on the street just before one o'clock to watch the Hemps ride in. Old Elihu rode in a buggy driven by one of the ranch hands. Behind him came a wagon, driven by another hand, that hauled one-legged Ferdie, busted arms Micah, and Ezra, sitting on a padded cushion. Other ranch hands and family rode on horseback. Emilie was not along. Lonzo, armed to the teeth, brought up the rear. They stopped in front of the Hard Luck Saloon, which would serve as a courtroom. The bar was closed. Watching the Hemps unload all their crippled was a sight to see. About the time the last of the Hemps got inside the makeshift courtroom, Slocum, Morton, Carl and Merilee came riding into town. The Hard Luck had never seen so many people crowded in at one time, and when it was filled to capacity, those who could not get in crowded around the batwing doors. In a few more minutes, Sheriff Hardy arrived with the judge, and the judge, whose name was Girty, took a place behind the bar. Using a pocket Merwin and Hulbert .38-caliber revolver as a gavel, he rapped on the bar for silence. Everyone shut up, and he called for the case. Hardy read off the charges.

"Are there any witnesses?" asked the judge. Sheriff Hardy pointed to Slocum and his three companions. "Bring one of them forward," Girty said.

Sheriff Hardy summoned Merilee to the bar, where she stood before the judge.

"What's your name?" he asked.

"Merilee Hornbuckle," she said. "Uh, Doaks."

The judge looked up at her quizzically. "Well," he said, "which is it?"

"I was Hornbuckle till I got married just yesterday," she said.

"So you're Doaks now, but at the time of the incident under question you were Hornbuckle. Is that correct?"

"Yes."

"Tell me about the incident."

"Well, it was way after dark, and me and Slocum was out at my house. We heard a bunch of riders coming, and we grabbed guns and run to the door. They went to shooting at us, and we shot back. They rode off, but Slocum shot one of them right in the ass."

"Watch your language in the courtroom, Mrs. Doaks," said Girty.

"Well, that's where he shot him."

"Proceed."

"That's all there is," she said. "We knowed that the Hemps was after my spread, and then we found out that Ezra was shot in the— What do I say, Your Honor?"

"You can say in the buttocks or in the behind," he said.

"Ezra was shot in the behind."

"That's it?"

"That's it."

"You did not recognize Ezra Hemp on the night of the shooting?"

"No."

"That's all. Call the next witness."

Sheriff Hardy motioned Slocum to come forward, and he did. "What's your name?" said the judge.

"Slocum."

"Your whole name."

"John Slocum."

"And you're the man that done the shooting?"

"That's right."

"You shot one of the raiders that was attacking the Hornbuckle place?"

"I did."

"Where'd you shoot him?"

"In the ass," said Slocum.

The judge cleared his throat. "Did you recognize the man at the time of the shooting?"

"No."

"Is there any more witnesses?"

"No, Your Honor," said Hardy. "There ain't."

"Then call Ezra Hemp up here."

Hemp was brought forward, limping and acting pitiful.

"Are you Ezra Hemp?" the judge asked.

"I am," said Ezra, whimpering a little bit for pity.

"Are you the man that was shot in the ass?" Girty said.

"I'm one of them," Ezra whined.

"What do you mean by that?" asked the judge.

"Well, Your Honor," whimpered Ezra, "I was out riding night herd one night about the time the Hornbuckle place was supposedly raided, and somebody shot me from ambush. He got away, and no one seen who done it."

"Is there any witnesses?"

"Yes, sir, a whole bunch of my family and our ranch hands was with me when it happened."

"You have no case here, Sheriff," said the judge. "There won't be no trial. Court's adjourned." He rapped on the bar with his pocket pistol. "Open the bar," he shouted. Elihu Hemp got up and moved forward. He waved at Brace the barkeep to fetch him over a bottle and glasses, and he poured two drinks, shoving one toward the judge.

"Thank you, Hiram," he said. He held up his drink.

Hiram Girty picked up his glass and touched it to Elihu's. "Justice has been served," he said. "Let's drink to justice."

Out on the sidewalk, a safe distance away from the jostling crowd, Gordy Glad stood with his two arms still tightly wrapped. He waited patiently for Jackson to emerge from the crowd and come over to his side.

"Well," he said, "what happened?"

"The judge said that there wasn't no case against Ezra Hemp," said Jackson.

Glad grinned. "That's good," he said. "When the crowd thins out a bit, we'll go inside and have a drink to celebrate Slocum's fortune."

After a couple of drinks in the bar, the Hemps left and loaded back up for the ride out to their ranch. Elihu invited Judge Hiram Girty to join them, and Girty rode beside Elihu in the buggy. "It's been a while since I've enjoyed your hospitality," he said. "It'll be a pleasure."

On the sidewalk, Slocum, Morton, Meilee and Carl watched them go. "See that," Merilee said. "Old Elihu and the judge is good friends. I knew it. I knew nothing would come of this goddamn hearing."

"The son of a bitch," said Morton.

"Watch your language," Merilee said.

"I don't think we've got anything to worry about," said Carl. "The Hemp crew is busted up so bad now that I believe old Hardy was right. They're whipped. They've quit."

"What do you think, Slocum?" Morton asked.

Slocum looked up just then to see Lonzo Hemp walking in their direction.

"I think any celebrating is a little premature," he said.

Lonzo strolled on over to stand in front of Slocum. He was wearing two six-guns strapped around his waist. There were two more in holsters on his chest. He squeaked when he walked, like saddle leather creaking.

"You're Slocum," he said.

"I know that."

"I'm Lonzo Hemp."

"Is there no end to you Hemps?" Merilee said.

Lonzo ignored her, as if she did not even exist. "Elihu said he was ready to call it quits," he said. "Well, I ain't. I mean to kill you, Slocum. Here and now or later somewheres else. A fair fight or an ambush. It don't make a damn to me. But I mean to kill you."

"Well, Lonzo," said Slocum, reaching down to unbuckle his gunbelt and hand it to Morton, "I've told all the rest of your kind that I didn't want to kill them. But I ain't going to say that to you. I think it'll be a real pleasure to kill you, you rotten son of a bitch."

Slocum's right fist snapped out and caught Lonzo on the side of the face, staggering him back. He almost fell, but he managed to keep his feet. His left hand automatically went for the gun at his left side. He had it halfway out of the holster before he realized what he was doing and stopped. He shoved it back in.

"Oh, no," he said, "I ain't falling for that."

He walked back up close to Slocum and swung a hard left which Slocum blocked with ease. He countered with a left to Lonzo's belly. Lonzo lost all of his air with a *whuff*. He doubled over. Slocum brought up a knee to Lonzo's face. Lonzo straightened up and staggered back again. His nose was bleeding. He wiped it with the back of his coat sleeve and snarled at Slocum. This time he moved in more cautiously, his guard up, his fists waving about in the air. He threw a fake left and then a fake right, and Slocum bobbed his head. Then Slocum faked a right, moving in close. He raised his right foot and brought it down hard, stomping on Lonzo's left foot with his boot heel, about as hard as he could stomp. Lonzo let out a howl that could be heard clear to the other end of Hard Luck. Slocum slugged him again with a right. This time Lonzo fell over on his back. This time he pulled a gun. This time Sheriff Hardy was right there with a shotgun in his hands.

"I wouldn't do that, mister," he said. Lonzo sat still for a moment. Then he put the gun away. "That man you're aiming to kill is unarmed," Hardy continued.

"He stomped my goddamned foot," said Lonzo, through clenched teeth. "Broke some bones, I imagine."

"I guess you ain't heard of him before, then," Hardy said. "We call him the Crippler."

"We ain't met, but I'd bet you're another Hemp. Is that right?"

"I'm Lonzo Hemp," Lonzo said, struggling to get to his feet. When he put weight on his left foot, he nearly fell again. "Shit," he said.

"Well, Lonzo Hemp," said Hardy, "I had me a talk with Elihu, and he told me that he was through with this fight."

"Elihu don't talk for me."

"He ought to. You're apt to wind up crippled permanent or killed. Have you thought about that?"

"I don't need no lectures, Sheriff."

"I guess not," said Hardy. "At least, I guess they won't

do no good. Well, do you want to finish this thing right here and now? You want Slocum to strap his gun back on and shoot it out with you? We'll have someone count to three and you both shoot. I won't arrest the winner. Not unless he pulls his gun before the count of three. You want to do that?"

"I'll pick the time," said Lonzo. "Right now my foot's hurting too bad."

"You don't shoot with your foot," said the sheriff. "You was fixing to shoot when I come up. What's wrong with now? You're packing four six-shooters, I see. Far as I know, Slocum just packs one. It ought to be more than a fair fight."

"Shut up and leave me be," snapped Lonzo. He turned and limped back toward his horse. Slocum, Merilee, Doaks, Morton and Hardy all watched him go. Morton started laughing. Merilee looked at Sheriff Hardy with curiosity.

"Hardy," she said, "I always thought that you was on their side. It looks like maybe I was wrong about you."

"Mrs. Doaks," said Hardy, "I tried to tell you all along that I wasn't on either side. I just try to enforce the law. When you told me that Hemp riders were raiding your cattle and your home, I believed you. I just didn't have any proof. You saw what happened in court today. The same would've happened any other time if I'd brought any of the Hemps in for trial. We just never had any proof."

Merilee looked at Carl. "Do you think we have time to buy the sheriff a drink, Carl?" she asked.

"I think so."

She looked from Slocum to Morton. "I suppose you two will join us?"

"I sure will," said Morton.

"Sure," said Slocum.

At last Merilee looked back at Hardy. "I never asked you," she said. "Can we buy you a drink?"

"Well, it'd be a pleasure," he said.

20

At the Hemp ranch house, Lonzo sat down in a big easy chair in Elihu's sitting room. Elihu sat behind his desk. A ranch hand was in the room with them, and Lonzo told the man to pull off his cousin's left boot, but when the man started to pull, Lonzo howled with pain. He reached under his big coat and pulled a long knife from a sheath at his belt.

"God damn it," he said, "I hate to ruin a good boot like this. That gives me one more good reason for killing Slocum."

He leaned over to begin slicing the boot off his foot.

"Lonzo," said Elihu, "I told the sheriff, I told Slocum, and I told you that I've quit this fight. I've give it up. You're making a liar out of me."

"All right, Elihu," said Lonzo, "so you've give it up. It ain't got nothing to do with you. This is between me and Slocum. That's all." He finished slicing the boot away from his foot and tossed it aside. "I need a pan of hot water," he said.

"I'll get it," said Emilie, and she left the room.

"Slocum will get his money tomorrow," Elihu said. "He'll get it and he'll leave these parts. Let it go."

"Tell you what I'll do, Cousin," Lonzo said. "I'll stop by

the sheriff's office, and I'll tell him that I don't work for you, and this thing is just between me and Slocum. That way you'll be in the clear. All right?"

Elihu let out a long sigh. Emilie came back into the room carrying a pan of hot water, which she set on the floor in front of Lonzo. Lonzo eased his left foot into the water with a groan.

"Bring me a paper and pencil," he said.

Emilie walked over to Elihu's desk to do Lonzo's bidding, but she did not like it. Not even Elihu talked to her like that. She handed the paper and pencil to Lonzo, who took it and began to write. When he was finished, he folded it in half.

"Where's that cowhand that like to've pulled my foot off?" he said.

"Hefty's just outside, I think," said Emilie. "You want him?"

"Yeah, I want him."

Emilie left the room. In another couple of minutes, Hefty walked in. He stepped over to the chair where Lonzo was sitting. "You want me?" he asked. Lonzo held out the paper toward Hefty.

"I want you to deliver this to Slocum," he said. "Right away."

Hefty glanced toward Elihu, and Elihu said, "Go ahead and do it." Hefty left the room.

"I wish I could talk you out of this," Elihu said.

"Forget it," said Lonzo. "It'll all be over with in the morning."

"You're going to have trouble with that Lonzo," said Sheriff Hardy.

"He didn't seem to be much trouble to me," Slocum said. They were sitting at a table in the Hard Luck Saloon—Slocum, Hardy, Morton, Carl and Merilee. They had already had one drink and were on their second. They were taking their time, sipping their drinks. No one intended on getting drunk. It was the middle of the afternoon.

"Slocum can handle him," Morton said.

"Well, he strikes me as the kind that will shoot you in the back," Hardy said. "I'd be careful."

"I'm always careful," Slocum said. "I'm still alive."

"Well, just you watch out for Lonzo Hemp. That's all I've got to say."

The Hemp cowhand called Hefty walked in the saloon just then. He spotted Slocum immediately and walked straight over to the table where Slocum and the others were sitting. He held the note out toward Slocum.

"I ain't here looking for trouble," he said. "I just come to deliver this message. That's all."

Slocum unfolded the paper. "It's from Lonzo," he said. "Where is he?"

"Last I seen of him," Hefty said, "he was setting in a chair in Elihu's room with his left foot in a pan of hot water." Morton laughed out loud. Hefty, feeling a little more comfortable then, said, "He had to cut off his boot with a Bowie knife." Morton, Carl and Merilee all laughed at that.

"What's the note say?" asked Hardy.

Slocum read the note out loud. "Slocum, I'll be in town in the morning. I'll be on horseback on the north end of town with my rifle ready. You come at me from the south end. Whoever shoots first, it'll be a fair fight."

"That's it?" said Hardy.

"That's it," said Slocum. He looked up at Hefty and said, "You can tell him I'll be here. Before you head back for the ranch, you might as well sit down and have a drink with us."

Hefty smiled. "Might as well," he said, and he pulled out a chair.

Just then Gordy Glad and Jackson walked in. They gave Slocum hard looks as they passed him by and found themselves a table. Jackson went to the bar and bought a bottle. He returned to the table with the bottle and two glasses, and he poured them both full. He took a long drink, and then he lifted the other glass and held it to Glad's lips. Merilee and Morton were watching, and they smiled at the sight. Glad glared back at them. At the table with Slocum, Hefty leaned across and spoke in a low voice.

"Is that the gunfighter you busted up?"

"That's Gordy Glad," Slocum said.

"Damn. He's in pitiful shape," Hefty said. "Can't even lift a drink."

"You can tell Lonzo Hemp," said Morton, "that he'll be lucky to wind up that well off."

"I'll tell him what I seen," said Hefty. "Damn, that's pitiful."

"Sheriff," said Slocum, "what time do you expect to have my money tomorrow?"

"It ought to be in the bank by ten o'clock."

Slocum faced Hefty again. "You can tell Lonzo that I'll be ready for him at ten-thirty." He looked back at the sheriff. "Is that all right with you? He said he's coming after me."

"I'll clear the streets," said Hardy.

The morning of Slocum's tenth day, Lonzo Hemp dressed, all but his left boot. He wrapped the wretched foot tight in strips of cloth. Then he checked all his weapons—four sixguns and a rifle. Using a gnarled stick for a cane, he hobbled out to his horse, which he had made Hefty saddle up for him, and he mounted up, leaving his left foot out of the stirrup. He headed for town.

Slocum was at Sheriff Hardy's office at ten o'clock. Hardy was not there, and Slocum figured that he was at the bank getting the money. He sat in a chair out on the sidewalk and waited. In a few minutes Hardy came walking back to the office. Slocum stood up and followed him inside. Hardy moved back behind his desk and sat down. He reached into a pocket and pulled out a wad of bills which he tossed on the desk in front of Slocum.

"Two thousand dollars," he said. "Count it."

Slocum picked up the wad and stuffed it into his own pocket. "I trust you," he said.

"Lonzo Hemp's at the far end of town waiting for you," said Hardy. "I cleared the streets. You can ride out the other direction, and he'll never find you."

"No," said Slocum. "I can't do that. Besides, he would find me. I'd just as soon get it over with right now."

"Suit yourself," said Hardy.

Slocum walked back outside. He stood on the sidewalk and studied the street. He could see no one. Hardy had indeed cleared the streets. He could not see Lonzo either. He was down there somewhere—waiting. Just then Slocum heard a rumble coming up from behind him, and he turned to see Elihu Hemp and some of his riders coming. Right behind him came Doaks and Merilee and Morton. He turned and opened the door to the sheriff's office. "Take a look out here," he said to Hardy. Hardy came out from behind his desk and went to the door. He saw the crowd coming. He stepped out on the sidewalk and waved them down.

"You all might as well wait in here," he said. "The saloon's already packed."

The Hemps and the Doakses all tied their horses and moved into the sheriff's office. As she passed by Slocum, Merilee paused. "Slocum," she said.

"Don't worry," he said.

"Slocum'll do all right, Sis," said Morton. They went on inside and crowded around the windows. Slocum stepped down into the street. He untied his big Appaloosa and swung up into the saddle. He turned the horse toward the north. He pulled out his Winchester and cranked a shell into the chamber. He nudged the horse forward, moving slowly down the street, watching both sides, looking at every corner.

Lonzo was sitting on his horse around the corner of the last building on the north end of Hard Luck. He had his rifle out and a shell in the chamber. He peered around the corner and saw Slocum headed in his direction. At the same time, Slocum saw the horse. With his good right foot, Lonzo kicked his horse into a sudden run and came out all at once, yelling and screaming and riding hard toward Slocum. He raised his rifle to his shoulder and snapped off a shot which whizzed above Slocum's head. He cranked another shell into the chamber and raised the rifle and fired again. This one took the hat off Slocum's head.

Slocum stopped riding. The Appaloosa stood still. Slocum raised his rifle and took careful aim. He fired, and his shot broke Lonzo's right shoulder. Lonzo shrieked and dropped his rifle. With his left hand, he pulled a revolver out of its holster and raised it to fire, but with no hands to hold on with and only one foot in a stirrup, he lost his balance and fell out of the saddle. The horse rushed on. Slocum dismounted. He sheathed his rifle and started walking toward the fallen Lonzo. Lonzo raised up as best he could. He lifted up the six-gun and fired a wild shot at Slocum. The distance was too great. The shot went wide. He fired again. Again he missed.

Slocum continued walking. He still did not have his Colt in his hand. "Give it up, Lonzo," he shouted. Lonzo's answer was another shot. This one kicked up dust in front of Slocum. Slocum stopped and stood still. Lonzo fired again and again and again. Frustrated, he tossed aside the weapon and drew another. Still Slocum did not move. Lonzo struggled to get to his feet. When he put weight on his left foot, pain shot through his body. The pain in his right shoulder had not yet kicked in. His shoulder was just numb. Standing uneasily, he raised the six-gun and fired. Slocum stood still. The shot went wide.

Inside the saloon, Jackson and Glad were pressed against one of the front windows. The crowd was pressed around and behind them, everyone wanting to get a good look. "What the hell is he doing?" Jackson said.

"He's playing it smart," said Glad. "They're too far apart for pistol shots."

Outside, Lonzo fired again. Slocum stood still. Lonzo fired again. "Come on closer, Slocum," Lonzo cried. Impatient, he fired once more. Slocum did not move. Lonzo took a step forward. When he stepped on his left foot, he winced with pain. He raised his weapon and sent another shot in Slocum's direction. He could see it kick up dirt off to Slocum's right. He staggered a couple more steps toward Slocum and fired again. Another wide shot. Still Slocum stood in place. He had not drawn out his Colt as yet. Lonzo tried again. His revolver was empty, and he tossed it aside and pulled out his third one. He staggered toward Slocum.

Slocum's right hand suddenly flashed to his Colt, and the Colt spat fire. Hot lead tore into Lonzo's right knee, and Lonzo's legs buckled. He fell to the dirt, dropping his six-gun at the same time. Slocum cocked his Colt and walked forward. Lonzo fumbled for his fourth and last six-gun. His face was twisted in pain and hate and was dripping sweat. "Leave it alone, Lonzo," said Slocum.

"And be like my cousins?" said Lonzo. "All crippled? Hell no."

With his left hand, Lonzo pulled out his last gun. He raised it and cocked it, and Slocum fired, his bullet drilling Lonzo's heart clean. Lonzo jerked and fell back dead. Slocum walked up to the body to make sure. He holstered his Colt and turned to walk back to his waiting horse. Morton was the first one out of the sheriff's office, but he was followed close by Carl and Merilee. Sheriff Hardy came close behind them. The Hemps came out of the office and walked straight for their fallen cousin. None looked in Slocum's direction.

"I knew you could do it, Slocum," Morton said.

"You gave him every chance," Merilee said. "The dumb son of a bitch."

Doaks slapped Slocum on the shoulder. "Good going, pard," he said.

Slocum ejected the two spent shells from his Colt and

reloaded. Then he holstered the Colt again. He looked at Sheriff Hardy.

"You're clean," Hardy said. "Lonzo came looking for the fight."

"No hearing?"

"Nope."

"Then I'll buy you all a meal before I leave town."

As they walked to the eating place, they saw the Hemps load the body of Lonzo into Elihu's buggy and head out of town.

"Do you reckon it's really over with?" said Morton.

"Elihu's whipped," said Hardy. "It's over."

They went inside the eating place and sat down. When the man came to take their order, even though it was a little early, they ordered the best lunch to be had. Waiting for their meals to be delivered, Merilee said, "Slocum, I don't know what we'd have done if you hadn't come along."

"It was all a plumb accident," said Hardy. "The way I see it, Slocum just saw a chance at a reward and took it. He didn't even know the Hemps had a stronghold here."

"That's right," said Slocum. "If I'd've known, I wouldn't have even tried to take Asa."

"And what about ole Hardy here," said Merilee. "I thought he was a son of a bitch, but by God I was wrong."

Everyone laughed at that. When they stopped laughing, Hardy said, "Thank you for that, I think."

Their meals were delivered, and the talk mostly stopped while they ate. They washed it all down with several cups of coffee. When they were finished, Slocum paid for it all. They walked out into the street, and Slocum moved toward his horse. He climbed into the saddle and tipped his hat.

"Do you have to go, Slocum?" said Morton.

"I'm afraid so," Slocum said. "I've done too much damage around this town. Got to find a fresh place and lay low."

21

Slocum could easily have stayed in Hard Luck, in a comfortable hotel room, and enjoyed another good meal or two and some good whiskey in the saloon, but he chose to leave it all behind him as soon as he possibly could. Hard Luck had been a bad experience, and he was glad to have it all behind him. All except for the two thousand bucks. That felt good in his pocket. He had no real idea where he was going, but he knew that he would find some towns to the west, and so that was the direction he headed. He smoked a good cigar as he rode easily along the trail. He was in no hurry. He had no obligations. No place he had to be. He had plenty of money to last him for quite a while if he did nothing too foolish with it. Something would turn up somewhere along the way.

When the sun started to get low in the western sky, Slocum decided to look for a place to camp. An early camp would be all right. That way, he could have a good look at the lay of the land and pick a good spot for the night. There was no hurry. He came at last to a stream of clear running water with a small grove of trees beside it. There was plenty of grass there for the Appaloosa. He decided to stop there. He unsaddled his stallion and let it loose in the grass near the stream. He built a small fire and rolled out his blankets beside it. He fixed himself a small trail meal and some coffee and enjoyed a leisurely feed. He drank an extra cup of coffee before turning in for the night. He had no worries. Everything was just fine.

Slocum was sleeping soundly when the unexpected voice woke him up. It was in the dead of the night. His fire had burned low, almost out.

"Wake up, Mr. Slocum."

He opened his eyes and squinted, and he found that he was looking into the double barrels of a greener.

"Jackson," he said, when he recognized the wretch behind the gun. Then he saw behind Jackson, sitting on a horse, Gordy Glad, his arms still wrapped tight. "What the hell are you doing?"

"Jackson's no gunfighter, Slocum," said Glad, "but with a shotgun, you don't have to be."

"I can blow your head right off," said Jackson, with a wheeze.

"Why would you want to do that?"

"For my boss, Mr. Glad there. For what you done to him. Maybe for five hundred dollars from Mr. Elihu Hemp."

"Those are pretty sorry reasons to die," said Slocum.

"You're the one who's about to die," said Glad. "You'd be dead already, but I wanted you to know who did it, and why."

"Well," said Slocum, "you might have had this ignorant son of a bitch clean the damn gun first."

"What?" said Jackson.

"It's clean enough," said Glad.

"What have you been doing with that thing?" Slocum said. "Using it for a crutch?"

"What do you mean?" said Jackson.

"Shoot him," said Glad.

"What do you mean a crutch?" said Jackson.

"You got the barrels all jammed with dirt," Slocum said. "You pull that trigger, you'll blow your own damn fool head off."

"He's lying," said Glad. "Kill him."

"You're lying," said Jackson. "I ain't stupid."

Then Jackson started to cough. The shotgun barrel roved around this way and that as he hacked and jerked with the fit. Slocum carefully found the Colt that was concealed underneath his blanket. He eased back the hammer. Jackson at last stopped coughing. Tears ran down his face. He pointed the shotgun back at Slocum's face.

"If I was you," Slocum said, "I'd at least turn that gun around and look in the barrels before I did anything stupid."

"Don't listen to him," said Glad. "Just shoot."

Slowly Jackson backed away from Slocum. Slowly he turned the gun to look into the barrels. "I can't see nothing," he said. "It's too dark."

Slocum pulled his Colt out from under the blanket and fired one shot. It tore into Jackson's heart. He dropped dead.

"Damn it," said Glad. "God damn it."

Slocum got up and walked over to where Glad sat helpless on his horse. He reached up to take hold of Glad's jacket and dragged him out of the saddle.

"What are you doing?" said Glad. "Do you mean to kill me?"

"I'd never kill a defenseless man," said Slocum. He picked up the shotgun where it had fallen when Jackson was shot. He pointed it into the air and fired, and Glad's horse and the one Jackson had been riding both took off.

"What are you doing?" said Glad.

"What do you know?" said Slocum. "The gun was all right."

He picked up his saddle and got his horse ready to ride. Then he rolled up his blankets and cleaned up the campsite. The last thing he did was kick out the remains of the small fire.

"What are you doing?"

Slocum mounted his Appaloosa. He looked down at Glad, standing alone and helpless out on the prairie, both his arms in slings, both elbows tightly wrapped, both hands bandaged till they looked like clubs.

"Gordy," Slocum said, "you should have let well enough alone. You had a man to wait on you. Now he's dead, and you're out here by yourself with no horse. I wonder how long you'll last."

He started to ride away. Glad screamed at him. "Slocum. You can't do this."

Slocum looked back over his shoulder. "Maybe those two horses didn't run too far," he said. "You might be able to catch up to one of them. Course, I don't know how in hell you'll get yourself into the saddle."

As Slocum disappeared into the darkness, Glad yelled out, "Slocum. God damn you. Slocum. You goddamned crippler."

Watch for

SLOCUM AND THE MESCAL SMUGGLERS

327th novel in the exciting SLOCUM series
from Jove

Coming in May!

JAKE LOGAN
TODAY'S HOTTEST ACTION WESTERN!